MYSTICAL ALLEY GROOVE

MYSTICAL ALLEY GROOVE

SCIONS OF MAGIC™ BOOK TWO

TR CAMERON   MICHAEL ANDERLE   MARTHA CARR

DISRUPTIVE IMAGINATION™

LMBPN Publishing
PMB 196, 2540 South Maryland Pkwy
Las Vegas, NV 89109

First US edition, December, 2019
Version 1.01, February 2020
ebook ISBN: 978-1-64202-618-4
Print ISBN: 978-1-64202-619-1

MYSTICAL ALLEY GROOVE TEAM

Thanks to the Beta Readers
John Ashmore, Nicole Emens, Kelly O'Donnell, Larry Omans

Thanks to the JIT Readers

Dave Hicks
Jeff Eaton
Deb Mader
Kathleen Fettig
Diane L. Smith
Dorothy Lloyd
Paul Westman

If I've missed anyone, please let me know!

Editor
Skyhunter Editing Team

DEDICATIONS

Dedication: For those who seek wonder around every corner and in each turning page. And, as always, for Dylan and Laurel.

— TR Cameron

CHAPTER ONE

C aliste Leblanc thrust a vicious jab at the throat of the
tall, dark-skinned man across from her. It traveled
toward him at a snail's pace and the muscles in her arm
trembled visibly. His block was equally slow, and a look of
dramatic horror spread over his face at the realization that
it wouldn't be in time to block the punch.

The crowd chuckled, then laughed harder at her
theatrical expression of triumph. Bills and coins landed in
Dasante's black top hat, which rested on the ground
between them and the audience. The scene ended with her
fist an inch from his throat and his eyes closed in defeat
before they turned together, clasped hands, and bowed.

Frozen fighting was one of her favorite acts, and in the
week or so of normalcy that had followed her adventures
with the gangs and the uneasy truce that resulted from
them, she'd spent time teaching Dasante how to be her
partner. Before, she'd always included whoever was available, but D had learned enough of her secrets that he had

1

become something more to her than he had been. He'd always been a friend but now was a confidant.

He sat on the ground beside the hat, wiped the sweat from his brow, and pushed his wavy black hair away from his face. Even in cargo shorts and a t-shirt, the blazing sun and the under-appreciated level of effort necessary to move so slowly had clearly drained him. Her t-shirt—advertising a David Bowie album cover—was noticeably damp as well above cut-off jean shorts.

She turned her head at a series of barks nearby and stared at the illusion-veiled Draksa, who appeared to be a Rottweiler rather than the similar-sized Dragon Lizard he truly was. Apparently, a bird nesting in one of the trees on the opposite side of the Jackson Square fence had done something to offend him. "Knock it off, Fyre."

He gave her one of his looks—the kind where she could see the mocking expression of his true form shining through the illusion—and continued to bark. Dasante laughed. "I don't think he's interested in listening to what you have to say."

Cali shook her head. "No one is, really. And it's sad because I'm so damn smart."

Her busking partner chuckled at her self-aggrandizing tone and retrieved the hat. He split the take equally and handed her coins and folded bills. "It wasn't a bad crowd today."

"It was decent. Where are Jen and Jax?" The duo usually performed on this side of the square facing Decatur but was conspicuously absent.

He shrugged. "They haven't been around for a few days

but didn't say they were going anywhere. No news has come to my ears."

She frowned. Ever since her discovery of the battle for territory taking place in the city, every strange fact that entered her radar made her wonder if it was a symptom of the conflict. It was still slow-moving enough that it hadn't registered with most people. If they noticed, it was only to cross the street to avoid the occasional tough-looking group acting like wherever they might be at a given moment belonged to them.

"It's probably nothing but still, it's worth keeping an eye out. Maybe ask around if you see any of their friends." Buskers looked out for each other. She'd always pictured the community as a giant team with individual members constantly trying to one-up each other. Overly competitive folks usually didn't last long among them. "Let me know if you do."

His head swiveled sharply toward her. "Do you think it means something?"

Cali sighed and stretched her legs out in front of her. The morning session with Sensei Ikehara had been a little more intense than usual, and she definitely felt it. "There's no way to tell. I'm probably only paranoid."

When he grinned, his white teeth were a notable contrast to his dark skin. "It doesn't mean they're not after you."

The easy comfort they had with each other was never better expressed than in the fact that they could tell one another the dumbest jokes and be assured of a positive result. "Who wouldn't want to be after this, really?" She gestured at her tanned skin and entirely average figure, which drew a laugh from her companion. Cali wouldn't win any beauty contests but she was fully comfortable in her own flesh, which was made for running, fighting, and working. *Speaking of which....* She pushed to her feet with a groan. "I've gotta head back and get ready for work."

Fyre barked again and ran to her side, clearly in support of the idea. He'd joined her at the tavern during her shifts, hanging out quietly behind the bar with her boss, Zeb. She was fairly sure the dwarf was feeding him stuff he shouldn't eat while she was busy serving the customers. It didn't seem to harm him, though, so she wasn't about to object. Anything that made two of her favorite people—well, beings—happy couldn't be bad.

Dasante laughed at the illusory dog. "I guess he gets bored easily, huh?"

She grinned. "Maybe we should include him in the next performance. He can chew on your foot."

"Good plan, as long as it's your foot instead."

As she moved toward him for the secret handshake they'd adopted, two shouts from farther down the sidewalk stopped her in her tracks. A busker painted gold and wearing a matching wedding dress stood over her partner, who sported the same colors on his skin and tuxedo and lay in an awkward position on the ground.

The woman yelled, "Hey, get back here, thief!" A bald man in a ratty t-shirt and jeans scrambled across the traffic with a gold purse in his hand.

Cali ran to the downed golden groom with Fyre at her heels and reached him as he regained his feet. "Rip and run?"

He nodded, and his partner said, "It's not a big deal. I was surprised but there is only a couple of days' worth in there." Her face suggested it was a bigger thing than her words described.

She growled annoyance. "I'll get him."

They both shook their heads. "You don't need to. We'll be fine."

Her glance slid to Fyre, who stared after the running thief with his muscles trembling. As always, she was glad to see they were of like mind. "I know you will. Right after we teach that jerk a lesson. No one gets away with that kind of nonsense when I'm around." The Draksa dashed forward toward where the man had disappeared into the trees near Café du Monde, and she pounded after him.

The moment they rounded the corner into the parking area behind the restaurant, Fyre launched himself up to the roof of the long building. She muttered and increased her pace. Without him to lead her, she'd have to get into the visual range of the thief, who was currently halfway down the row of cars. *Damn, he's fast. I wonder if he's using magic?* Discovering whether her own powers could be used to increase her speed or strength was on her magical to-do list, but it was fairly far down in the ranked priorities. When he vaulted a low wall and scrambled back toward the city, she lost sight of him again. She lowered her head and pushed forward at her top velocity.

Cali skidded around the corner on Dumaine Street and narrowly avoided a collision with a group of laughing pedestrians who made their way from the nearby trolley stop. The flash of her quarry's red shirt on the other side of the road and to the right caught her eye in the same moment that Fyre glided over her head toward the rooftop diagonally across the intersection. She assumed he had veiled himself since most of the passersby stared at her rather than the small dragon or Rottweiler that soared over them.

Her path was blocked by a tall iron gate when she entered the narrow alley. Three-story-high buildings lined it to the left, and a two-story wall made up the right side. She caught hold of the bars and yanked, knowing it would be locked but needing to try anyway. With a sigh, she climbed and used force blasts to carry her the final foot over the sharp points on the top and prevent her from major impact with the ground below. She landed hard, rolled, and came up running again. Irritation surged through her at the new tear in her t-shirt.

An opening yawned ahead on the right, and she was about to curl into it when Fyre roared a warning. She slid instead, unable to arrest her momentum, and heard the staccato barks of a pistol and the sound of the bullets whistling over her head. Her momentum careened her past the gap and she bounced up again, her bare legs scraped from the grinding contact with the rough asphalt of the alley. Counting on the unlikelihood of a street tough having the expensive ammunition that could ignore magic, she summoned a full-body force shield and held it before her as she darted around the corner.

He immediately unloaded several more shots into the

barrier, then seemed panicked as he turned again to run. The building ahead appeared to have been an industrial space before it was converted to apartments, and clothes hung on lines on the porches that covered the back wall. He disappeared into a door at the bottom, and she stalked carefully toward it. Fyre landed on the roof high above. She looked up and gave him a nod of approval. *He'll watch the outside so the jerk can't escape.* They'd decided that was the best strategy to avoid revealing his true nature if his veil slipped. She didn't want to play that card until it was truly essential. *It's time to explain to the idiot that stealing is bad.*

She pushed through the scratched metal barrier into a narrow hallway that ran to another door on the opposite wall. An opening between took up the middle of the building, and she crept warily forward to discover a staircase leading up on each side. She jogged partially up the one to the right, stuck her head out to peer upward, and caught a flash of red on the top floor. With another sigh, she followed carefully, speed no longer essential. *At times like this, I wish I had a radio to coordinate with Fyre. He could go in a window and chase the jerk out for me.*

Cali cleared the second level without incident but noticed a strange shimmer near the switchback halfway up toward the third. She slid her hands behind her back and commanded her red-etched black bracelets to become her magical Escrima sticks. They vibrated as energy flowed into them after the grips slipped into her palms, sipping her power to refuel for the next transformation. She kept her eyes defocused and her attention wide and detected the attack before it could strike. A blast of shadow magic met her crossed weapons and dissipated. She threw the left-hand stick at the source and an illusion dropped to reveal a man casting another spell at her.

She ducked and rolled forward under the burst of force magic that rippled the air over her head. Her body straightened in time to block the shadow knife he stabbed at her with a frantic swipe of her stick. The quarters were too close for planning and too close for anything other than immediate action. She planted her left fist in his stomach and the breath whooshed from him. A step back gave her room to kick, and she drove her foot up toward his groin.

He blocked it with a downward punch that hurt more than it should have—*force shield around the hand, ow*—and launched a back fist at her nose. With stairs behind her, all she could do was drop to the floor, and his follow-up knee strike connected with her shoulder and dislodged her right-hand stick. Unfortunately for him, her Aikido training emphasized groundwork.

Her hand snaked out to grasp his shin and she used it as a lever to pull herself around him, lock both his legs, and bring him down with one quick yank. Before he could react, his neck was trapped between her crossed calves and his air supply cut off. He battered at her, but his punches lacked power. When he managed enough brainpower to summon his magical blade again, she blocked it with a force shield. He passed out, and it was only when she released him that the true import of the short battle hit her mind.

This isn't the guy I was chasing. Which means he has friends, which means this is an ambush. A clatter as doors banged open above and below her position on the stairs confirmed her realization.

CHAPTER TWO

On the assumption that there were two floors' worth of potential adversaries behind her but only one above, Cali raced up the remaining half-flight of stairs and called her sticks back to her hands. She raised them in an X as she cleared the stairwell and intercepted an arc of lightning that coalesced around them before it vanished. "Nice trick."

The hoodie-wearing caster made no reply and merely launched another electrical barrage, this one aimed at the floor beneath her. She leapt to avoid the possibility of the boards collapsing beneath her feet and her trajectory took her toward her attacker. His magic crackled ominously but she cleared it easily it to land a short distance away from him. She broke into an immediate run and stabbed her left stick at his solar plexus as a feint before she swung the right one in a hard, lateral strike from outside.

He blocked the first with a downward swipe of his free hand and managed to place his opposite forearm in the way of the second. A loud crack signaled at least a fracture, and he howled in immediate pain. She used the moment of distraction to dispatch him with a front kick to the center of his body that stole his breath and dropped him into a crumpled heap. *Damn. I need to carry rope or a tranquilizer or something. One more thing on the to-do list.*

Her brief concern over how to ensure his non-participation in the rest of the fight was blown away by the force blast that caught her squarely in the back. She catapulted down the hallway but managed to raise her hands and twist her body in time to take the impact with the far wall —originally twenty feet distant—on her side rather than her face.

Cali fought against the continued pressure of the spell to position her sticks in the way, and as they crossed, the assault faltered. She slid down the wall to the floor, held her defense before her, and identified three attackers. The woman in the front wore a hoodie that was apparently the Atlantean gang's uniform, and her hair and skin were both dusky in the minimal light provided by the pair of bare bulbs hanging overhead. The defeat of her attack had brought a snarl to her face.

The other two both looked like men, although the cowls hiding most of their faces made it impossible to be sure. One of them held a baseball bat in a confident grasp and the other, dual long knives formed of shadow power. *So, they want it to be personal to send a message or some garbage. I'm down.* She lurched into motion, hurled her sticks forward at the woman to distract her, and summoned a force shield as she pounded down the hallway toward her foes.

Damn it. I really need magic that will make me faster. She was more a marathoner than a sprinter when it came down to it. The memory of Zeb telling her she had to pursue people who tried to dine and ditch at the tavern because dwarves were short-distance runners brought a grin that doubtless confused her opponents. Her force shield—a curved barrier that covered her from head to toe and wrapped around both sides—absorbed the woman's successive attacks. A subtle shift in positioning redirected them without fully absorbing their power, which allowed Cali to maintain her momentum and resulted in the destruction of several pieces of drywall from the deflected bursts.

She discarded potential attack possibilities one after the other during her charge and kept her options open until the last minute. When the other woman stepped back into a weak defensive stance, the choice was clear. Cali summoned a final burst of speed and drove the shield into her to thrust her foe toward the man with the knives. She shrank the magical defense to normal shield size and envisioned it attaching itself to her left forearm. Her right stick returned to her hand as she slid low toward the one holding the bat.

He grinned as he swung his arm back and adjusted his aim. The weapon descended in a powerful arc. Her trained eyes noted the balanced stance and how he pivoted from his hips and channeled the momentum into his swing. It was essentially an optimal strike with the club, and when her force shield met it, the energy of the blow traveled up her arm and made her shoulder ache. The problem with committing to the attack the way he had, though, was that it allowed no opportunity for defense. Her slide brought her heels in contact with his feet, compromised his balance, and forced him to lock his knees. She struck the outside of his left knee with her right-hand Escrima stick backed by enough force to dislocate it. He fell with a shriek as she rolled away.

As she stood, she darted a hasty glance down the stairs and saw four attackers charging upward. She growled in annoyance. "Sorry about this, buddy," she muttered and used her force magic to hurl her latest casualty toward them at chest height. He barreled into the oncoming enemies and they all tumbled back to the landing. Another force blast from the woman caught Cali in the left shoulder and thrust her to the side as the man with the daggers attacked. She swung her shield in front of the first blow but felt a line of fire across her stomach as the other blade sliced through her t-shirt and into the flesh beneath.

"Ow—bastard," she shouted and released the force shield as her second stick returned to her grasp. Her practice sessions with Ikehara had increased her speed dramatically, and she numbed his left wrist with a carefully aimed blow to the bone. The blade vanished, his concentration compromised. He brought the other one back in a reverse strike at her stomach, but she stepped away long enough to let it pass and drilled a sidekick into his ribs. She heard a crack, and he stumbled away with a gasp. Cali grinned at the woman, who had been reduced to a spectator during the close-quarters exchange, unable to attack without risking her own ally. "Bring it, witch." *It works on two levels, see, because you're a total jerk and also a female who can cast magic. I'm hilarious.*

Her opponent apparently didn't understand or appreciate the joke. When she attacked, it was with an enormous ball of fire that Cali barely managed to raise her sticks in time to intercept. The flames were momentarily sucked toward the weapons but immediately blew out in a wide arc. Heat washed over her bare legs but missed the rest of her. The pain didn't register immediately, but she knew it was only a matter of time. She'd been burned at work too many times to count—*stupid stew pot*—and knew that even a simple burn produced an agony far out of proportion to the damage. Grimly, she realized she was on the clock, as the potential for the impending pain to overwhelm her when it arrived was all too real.

The woman had followed the blast with a cone of fire that the sticks absorbed, and Cali walked forward against its pressure to narrow the distance between them. The throbbing in her legs grew more intense and drew a small whine from deep in her lungs. *Shut up. There's no time. Later.* She gritted her teeth and forced herself to ignore the sensation. Her foe trembled visibly as she poured her power into the attack, but it wasn't sufficient to stop her advance. The woman seemed shocked when the distance was finally short enough to allow a front kick to the groin to shatter her focus followed by a blow to the temple from one of her sticks that rendered her unconscious.

She realized belatedly that the sprinkler system had activated and she was drenched. Irritated, she pushed wet hair out of her eyes and looked for more opponents, but none were visible. She willed her sticks to return to their bracelet form, extended her hands, and ejected a cone of frost that reached toward the flames on the far wall to smother them. Her ears rang from the violence and the rushing water, but she could still make out the sound of oncoming sirens. She considered heading down the stairs but thought better of it when one of her legs buckled and she staggered.

Okay, then, if I can't go down, I guess it's up. It occurred to her that she was out of time to find the thief, so she took the money from the wallet of the woman in front of her. *At least I can give them something.* She limped toward the nearest door and blasted it apart with a ball of force. Her movements stiff and pained, she climbed through the hole she'd made and headed to the window opposite, down a hallway, and through the living room. She stuck her head out to discover that it wasn't the one she'd hoped for but saw the fire escape one room over. *Well, I got the correct side of the building.* She hurried into the bedroom and out through the window, taking the metal stairs slowly to the roof.

Fyre met her at the top with a smug expression. Two unconscious enemies near him revealed that they'd been prepared for her to go up and he'd dealt with them, presumably without betraying his true nature since they weren't covered in ice.

She asked, "Any problems?" He laughed and swayed his head from left to right.

The Draksa led her to the corner of the building. His always deeper than expected voice was concerned. "Can you make the jump?"

Cali peered over the edge to see the roof of the next structure a story below. The lateral distance wasn't an issue, but the drop might hurt. Of course, the alternative was to wait where she was and hope to not be discovered, which was totally unlikely. Her legs shook beneath her and she sighed. "No chance. We'll have to risk a portal."

He nodded and his snout lowered once. A rift appeared in the air beside her as she sagged from the strain of her burns, and she crawled through to safety in the tavern basement.

The stone floor beneath her cheek was comforting after the blazing heat of the apartment building, and the pain in her legs was powerful enough that she couldn't even think of moving. Fyre wasted no time and raced up the stairs. Moments later, her boss grumbled loudly, "What's she gone and done to herself now?"

The Draksa didn't answer, having decided for whatever reason his lizard brain thought important that he'd only speak to her and Tanyith. A rustling followed as if Zeb was rooting through one of the crates that were stacked all over the space before he eased her into a seated position. She groaned at the flood of pain, but when he tilted the healing potion to her lips, she drank greedily. In moments, the agony had abated, and she watched the scarlet skin and giant blisters fade from her legs. A strange tingle lingered as the slash on her stomach sealed itself and left her trembling again, this time with relief.

She sagged back against the dwarf. "Oh, that's so much better. Thank you."

His head shake was felt rather than seen. "You have to be more careful, girl. What happened?"

"Ambush. Atlanteans. I think I'll take a nap now." The

effects of the healing potion came at a price, and exhaustion washed over her.

He chuckled, guided her to the floor, and shoved a folded cloth of some kind under her head. "You have four hours until your shift starts. Enjoy your rest."

Cali managed to mumble "Brutal...taskmaster...jerk..." before her consciousness slipped away.

CHAPTER THREE

T anyith chuckled quietly. "I spend way too much time on this roof." He looked around at the barren surface and leaned back in the folding canvas chair he'd brought with him. A paper cup of cold coffee was half-full in its holder, and he grimaced at the thought of drinking any more. Across the street and several stories below, the Saturday night crowd flowed into the Shark Nightclub. There had been no sign of important members of the Atlantean gang so far, but he doubted they'd let the evening pass without someone making the rounds. He'd spent a large part of the previous week surveilling them, and patterns had emerged.

He sighed. "And now, I'm talking to myself. Great." The sight and sound shield around his perch would ensure that no one heard him, but it still wasn't a particularly good sign that his internal monologue had become external. Further consideration of the topic was forestalled by the opening of the garage door a block away. The fact that he and Cali had invaded the club by that route hadn't stopped them from employing the space. The dark sedan pulled out and he cursed as he ran to the back of the building.

Without hesitation, he jumped and used force magic to control his speed and land lightly beside the motorcycle parked there. This one wasn't "borrowed" as his previous ride had been but rather purchased secondhand. Even though he'd stashed money and supplies away before his involuntary trip to Trevilsom prison, he hadn't been willing to pay for a new one. The Yamaha SR was adequate and didn't stand out in the streets of New Orleans. He yanked on the black helmet and gunned the engine. Casually, he paralleled the car for a while and assumed it was on its way to the Quarter. When they neared that destination, he swung over and moved into position behind it, close enough to detect any turns or stops but sufficiently far back to avoid revealing himself.

It took twenty minutes of winding through pedestrians and traffic before the other vehicle stopped outside one of the other nightclubs in town that catered primarily to the magical crowd. The Witch's Cauldron looked like a tourist trap with its costumed servers and year-round Halloween decorations. But there were always people with real power scattered among them, and he'd heard tell of a VIP room somewhere inside. Of course, if it held a portal, the actual space for the elite could be an entire planet away.

He steered the bike to the side and as the rear doors of the car opened, he whispered a spell that would allow him to see the scene as if from only a few feet away. He nodded in a mixture of surprise and confirmation as the leader of the Atlantean gang, Usha, emerged from the back passenger seat. She wore a bright red dress that shimmered in the neon lights from the surrounding bars. It reached to her calves and obscured the tops of the black boots she wore. Her hair was pulled away from her face in a narrow braid that hung in a queue down her spine. She stopped to await the two other figures who climbed out of the opposite side of the vehicle.

The first was someone he hadn't seen before. He was stocky and a short beard darkened his tanned skin. His tight black t-shirt and matching jeans put his impressive muscles on display, and his gaze cast about warily. *I guess he's a bodyguard of some kind. He looks too tough to be local. So, he's imported from somewhere.* The woman who followed was instantly recognizable.

Danna Cudon was the second in command to the Atlantean leader. She was a formidable presence despite the distance between them. Her eyes were protected by stylish sunglasses, and her dark suit, shirt, and tie were perfect, as they always were. Even during battle, the woman's wardrobe had remained almost entirely unruffled. He shook his head at the memory of the wicked spear she'd created out of nothing and almost gutted him with. *If she's the backup, the leader must be something much more dangerous than she appears,* he thought, not for the first time.

It was a pleasure to watch her move as she strode after the bodyguard, who had reached his ward. They walked in a line into the club and vanished from view. Tanyith climbed off the bike and straightened his outfit. While a suit wasn't his primary choice for either surveillance or riding, the need to look the part of an appropriately formal carouser was something he'd anticipated after trailing people from the Shark on previous outings.

The bouncer stopped him at the door, but a smoothly transferred twenty-dollar bill got him through without any further restriction. Inside, loud music thumped at twice the rate of his heart, and flashing lights in every color of the rainbow whirled their beams through the fog of dry ice that floated around. The bar was to the left, a shining piece of metal that stretched from front to rear and reflected light in all directions. To the right was a doorway that presumably led to restrooms and back of house, and the rest of that wall was taken up by semicircular booths facing the interior. The remainder of the space, which seemed to be about four storefronts wide and at least half a block deep, was filled with a throng of dancers in varying states of visible drunkenness.

He caught sight of his prey in the distance, already most of the way through the crowd. With muttered apologies, he pushed through the people separating him from the Atlanteans. He lost ground with each passing moment as the bodyguard appeared to use his bulk to create space for the women. When he was almost sure they were headed to a VIP door he didn't know about, they made an unexpected turn to the right and stopped in front of one of the booths.

Tanyith stopped too, barely in time to avoid detection by the big man as he swept his gaze across the crowd. He chose a nearby woman at random and danced toward her. She either didn't notice or didn't care, but it made him look identical to all the other men striking out on the dance floor. He kept the disguise up through the end of one song and into the next and moved casually but consistently closer to the group. When he was about ten feet away, he saw the strange positioning of the people involved. The boss was talking to a man in the center of the curved booth, who was surrounded on both sides by women in sparkling cocktail dresses. The arrangement screamed "important person," but he didn't recognize anyone.

Of course, I've been out of commission for a while. There's no way to know who might have risen or fallen during my enforced absence. While the boss talked and the bodyguard scanned the crowd, motion from Danna Cudon caught his eye. The woman flicked her wrist strangely, and he was virtually positive he saw a flash of white in her fingers before she grasped the extended hand of the woman closest to her. She maintained the grip for longer than necessary, and first interest and then trepidation flashed across the sparkling woman's face. He noted in passing the pointed ears that betrayed her Oriceran ancestry. Then, her hand was free and the Atlantean second repeated the process with each of the women at the table.

Her last shake was with the man, and it finished with a dip of her hand into her inside jacket pocket, which sealed the deal for Tanyith. She'd provided something to the women, at least, and had received payment from the man. *What could it be? Secrets? Stolen goods? Drugs?* His mind latched onto the last as the most likely option. It was one of the things he'd argued against when he was part of the group. Two of the things, actually, as there had been a plan to deal drugs that only affected humans and another to provide ones to the magical community. If he was right, the latter was definitely in play. Time would tell regarding the former.

The Atlanteans suddenly lurched into motion, turned,

and plunged into the crowd. Tanyith danced toward the bar and did his best to look like a man seeking a drink, then followed at a discreet distance. When he saw the dark car pull away, he darted out of the entrance and ran to his bike. It was only dumb luck that let him catch up to them, thanks to a drunken reveler in the middle of the street who had slowed traffic to a crawl.

He tracked them to several more bars, but only Danna got out so he didn't risk following her inside. At the end of the night, the car returned to the Shark and Usha exited, followed immediately by her burly, bearded guardian. The sedan pulled away, and his expectations proved inaccurate as it continued past the garage. *What are you up to now?* He trailed it again, paranoid that the strange trip was a trap of some kind. His quarry took a direct route through the city that ending at a luxurious apartment building on the opposite side.

A block away, he watched as she left the car and entered the structure. He made a note of the location on his phone while he tried and failed to suppress a yawn. Half his instincts told him to stay and watch and the other half replied that doing so would be stupid, as she was almost certainly in for the night. He finally settled on the side of the latter and turned his motorcycle toward the cheap by-the-week apartment he currently called home.

Thoughts flitted across his mind as he rode—his worries about the gang, discovering what was going on in New Atlantis, and finding a job before his money ran out were sufficient to keep him awake during the long trip back to his bed.

CHAPTER FOUR

Sunday morning dawned cloudy and rainy, a rare occurrence in the Crescent City. Fyre made the area around the bed increasingly cold until Cali climbed grumblingly out of the sheets and agreed to go for a run with him. She changed and opened the door to confirm that her path down the stairs was clear.

Her relief lasted only until the moment when Mrs Jackson stepped out of nowhere to appear at the bottom. "Caliste." Her voice was filled with disapproval.

She kept the sigh from reaching her lips. "Yes, Mrs. J?"

The boarding house's owner was a woman from another era. She had never seen her in anything but a dress, usually with far too many fasteners up the front to be practical. Today, it was a black one with white buttons and a small hat covered her grey hair. *That's right, it's Sunday.* She wasn't sure what church her landlady belonged to, but the woman never missed a week. The old lady folded her arms. "You were out awfully late. I heard you come in."

Since I portaled in, there's no damn way you heard me. Isn't lying a sin? She plastered a regretful smile on her face. "I had to work until closing at the restaurant." Mrs J disapproved of the word "tavern" and all its assorted connotations. It was easier to simply not bring it up.

She felt cold against her leg as Fyre snorted almost silently behind her. The older woman suggested, "Maybe you should find a less…late-night kind of job." It was as close as she came to outright accusing her of being a person of loose morals, but the subtext was there and not buried particularly deep.

"You know that the owner's a friend of my family." Mentioning her loss never failed to put her landlady off track.

"Oh, yes, your poor parents. I can't imagine what they'd make of you now." There was a pause and like she had many times before, Cali considered letting it stretch to see how long it could last. The impatient Draksa at her heels made that a bad idea on this occasion, at least, so she simply walked forward with a wave. Mrs Jackson called after her, "Don't forget to lock up behind you. I keep hearing strange things in the house and it makes me nervous."

"Yes, Mrs J," she yelled in reply and after she'd closed the door behind her, she whispered, "I think she's talking about you."

Fyre's voice didn't contain the mischievousness she'd expected. "I am not strange."

She chuckled. "Only a little, maybe." He failed to rise to the bait, and she shrugged and broke into a jog. He trotted beside her as she warmed up, then pushed her to go faster by racing ahead. They remained in the neighborhood and zig-zagged along each street, then turned in the opposite direction to return. In fifteen minutes, her legs hurt and after thirty, her muscles burned. She found a grassy island on one of the nicer streets and sank into the wet grass, willing to endure a little damp in return for a chance to rest her muscles.

Fyre sat primly and seemed to stare at her. She tilted her head to one side. "What's up with you?"

She'd never seen confusion on his face before, and it was momentarily shocking. His voice was pensive. "Have you ever felt like there was something you needed to remember—something fundamental—that simply wouldn't come?"

It was easy to forget he wasn't an ordinary animal companion from time to time. He liked to act the pet and hung out behind the bar, napped curled up near her when she was at home, and even played when the mood struck him. But there was no question that the Draksa was far more than that.

Cali nodded. "Yeah, I have. After my parents were killed, I woke up every night for half a year thinking that if I could remember some key thing, I could undo it. Like it was all a dream simply awaiting my revelation to avoid it becoming a part of the real world. Of course, it wasn't true, but it felt like it was. It still does, sometimes."

He nodded. His scales were even more metallic and reflective than they had been when she'd met him, which indicated that he had moved closer to the male end of the Draksa gender spectrum. At least she thought that was what it meant. The dragon was a mystery to her, most days. *And maybe that's part of the problem.* He spoke with a continued lack of confidence that sounded wrong coming from him. "I don't really remember anything before the graveyard. Do you think that's weird?"

She frowned. "I guess I'm not sure. Emalia said Draksa hatch from eggs, so it's certainly possible that someone put your egg in the graveyard. It doesn't seem likely, though. She gave me the impression that your species was rare and special, and simply leaving an egg in a random place wouldn't make much sense. You are, of course, the proof of the rare specialness of the Draksa."

His tongue hung out momentarily in what she'd come to understand as a sarcastic grin, but he soon resumed his troubled look. "I doubt we emerge from the egg at this size. So, what happened between the one and the other? Why can't I remember?"

In a gesture of companionship, she ran her hand down his flank and marveled at the feel of his scales beneath her fingertips. The ones that looked metallic felt like it, too, and the others were similar to a lizard's skin, soft and mostly smooth. Fyre pressed into her palm like a cat, and she was silent while she considered what to say. He seemed comfortable with the delay or at least soothed by the attention. Finally, her thoughts coalesced into something useful. "Zeb told me, after my parents were gone, that I couldn't live my life worrying about what had happened, or what might have been, or what could occur in the future. The past no longer matters, he said, except as the path we took to the present. Its echoes linger but shouldn't be allowed to change the now. Today is all we can really be sure we have."

Fyre snorted. "That sounds like something he'd say."

She laughed. "I think he gets most of his wisdom from watching the kung fu channel, but every now and again, he makes sense." With a groan, she stretched, grabbed her feet, and pulled her head down to her knees. Without looking at him, she added quietly, "If hanging out with me doesn't make you happy, you should find something that does."

"It's definitely not that. If anything is lacking, it can't be filled from outside. I only wish I could remember. At least then I'd know if it was really something or if I'm worrying about nothing."

She shook her head in sympathy. "I've been there, my friend. You simply need to keep moving forward. Everything will turn out as it should."

"Zeb?"

"No. Caliste." She groaned again as she pushed herself to her feet. "While we're talking about important things, it's time we started putting all that talking about training together into action. I discussed it with Emalia, and a couple of days a week, she'll shorten the magic lessons so you and I can put some practice in. You need to teach me how to fight properly beside a Draksa."

"I can share what I remember."

"How much is that? What do you think is missing?"

He paused to scratch his pointed ears with a back paw before he replied. "I remember the big things. Fighting. Hunting. Mating."

She raised a hand, palm out. "Too much information. Stick to the first two."

His laugh emerged as something between a sibilant human laugh and a bark in his native form. "But I recall so much about the third." His snout wrinkled as he shook his head. "We will definitely need to fight side by side, rather than front and back. Your instincts appear to drive you directly into the teeth of the enemy."

Cali nodded. "Yeah. There's some truth to that. So at least we have a rough plan." Something he'd said triggered a thought. "How old are you, anyway?"

A frown replaced his neutral expression. "I don't know. I'm not a youngling but not an elder. Somewhere in between."

She started to jog again, and he loped into position beside her. She kept the pace slow enough that she could still talk. "It does seem like you're missing some important memories. We could ask Emalia what she knows about Draksa."

"Or Zeb."

"Hey, now there's an idea. Let's ask Zeb."

After a rare afternoon spent indoors doing homework for her Criminal Behavior Theory class, Cali and Fyre reported for work early via portal. *Well, I'm reporting for work. He's reporting for sleeping behind the bar and being spoiled.* They climbed the stairs from the basement to discover Zeb cleaning and prepping for the evening crowd. His movements were quick and sure as he polished furniture and arranged items on the tables according to his standards of perfection. The scent of the night's stew wafted up from the cook pot, and the heavy peppery smell made her eyes water. Fyre sneezed and announced their presence.

Zeb smiled at them from the middle of the tavern. "Feel free to grab a rag and work on those muscles. The bar could use a polish."

She shook her head. "No thanks. I have to save my energy for my actual job." She hopped up on one of the high seats along the already gleaming bar. "What do you know about Draksa?"

He paused and looked from her to Fyre. "Am I really the right person to ask?"

"Humor me."

"They are Atlantean," he said with a shrug. "Part dragon, part lizard. The females lay eggs, which lie dormant for a long time. If you're dumb enough to get in a fight with one and you're super lucky, it might bond with you rather than killing you."

Cali rolled her eyes. "You're truly a wealth of knowledge. Do you have anything else?"

The dwarf adjusted a final item and strode toward the bar. She often wondered how he managed his effortless speed with such short legs but had long since decided that asking would either get her made fun of or ignored. So, naturally, she merely waited for the right moment to ask, the one that would cause him the most irritation—probably when the place was filled with customers. "Okay, let's see. They have the ability to change genders during their lives, but not all do. And they're accomplished hunters. They have different magics—some use frost, some fire, and there's even been a rumor or two of shadow Draksa out there somewhere. Their personality runs along the same continuum as yours or mine, as do ethical stances. Some are good and some less good."

He scratched his beard once he'd stepped beyond the pass-through and behind the bar, then started to arrange glasses. "Some people say that the bonding changes each member and adds the other's positive qualities." He looked at her with a twinkle in his eye. "For instance, you've seemed smarter after meeting Fyre. Perhaps he's rubbing off on you."

She made a stupid face and stuck her tongue out to the side. "Ha, ha, ha." She shook her head. "So you know nothing about how they grow or anything?"

He shrugged. "I assume it's the same as all of us. They start smaller and get bigger."

"But they live a long time, right?"

"Longer than some but shorter than others. About the same as a human is what I've read."

"There are books?"

The dwarf laughed. "Of course there are books." He shook his head. "It took you long enough to ask. I've waited...what is it, eight months now? I assumed Emalia would have sent you to the library long ago."

She folded her arms. "I'm not an idiot. I've been to the library. My school has one too, you know."

Zeb sighed. "The magical library, doofus." He looked at his ornate watch—which reminded her of a steampunk Halloween costume accessory she'd seen in the Quarter—and changed the subject. "Right. You're on the clock, girl. Get to work."

Cali groaned and crossed to the front door, threw the locks, and opened it to reveal a gaggle of wizards, each of whom carried a small bag. With another groan, she realized that tonight must be the monthly game night, which always resulted in nothing but chaos. She pointed at her boss as she headed to the stew pot. "Magic toys and alcohol don't mix. Why do you keep doing this to us?"

"Because it's fun." He grinned. "Embrace the moment, Caliste." He retrieved his own bag from under the bar and went to join his early arrivals for a game.

CHAPTER FIVE

Usha Serris lay back on the new couch in her redecorated office and closed her eyes. She was in a decidedly good mood. Despite the setbacks of a week before, everything was once again in its proper place. The broken piece of the legendary artifact sword was in a better hiding place, the demand for their newest product was high, and her people were working on a version that would appeal to—and quickly addict—humans as well. All in all, the Atlanteans in New Orleans were moving in the right direction.

Except for a few and most notably, Tanyith and his young partner, Cali. Their use of magic to infiltrate the club had invalidated their human gang disguises and left little doubt that they were the ones responsible. The sometimes-invisible dog at their side had been a different breed than the one the girl had been seen with before, but that could easily have been an illusion too. She chuckled quietly. *A stupid one. It would have been better not to bring the animal at all. But they must have known we'd see through the disguise.*

She gave them credit, though, for such a bold move. It was surely only dumb luck that had revealed the shard to them, but it had provided enough leverage to protect several businesses in addition to the dwarf's tavern. *For now.* She wouldn't go back on her word until the human leader of the Zatoras broke the truce since it would be unproductive to have the city's other magicals ranged in opposition to her. But she certainly wasn't above pushing to make him crack first.

That was the big picture, and it was all rosy. The small picture was the duo of meddlers, and that needed to be addressed. Ambushing the girl hadn't been well planned, and the underlings who had decided not to seek permission before they acted were now in the human penal system, arrested by the detective who'd been seen frequenting the tavern. Nothing happened around that building anymore without her knowledge, thanks to a rotating set of watchers. They also disabled the surveillance cameras that constantly appeared nearby, presumably placed by the Zatora syndicate.

A small chime sounded over the speakers hidden in the walls, and she opened her eyes and rose to her feet in a smooth motion. The room had been repainted in blues and greens and the shading suggested waves and light filtering through water. The couches were new leather and still smelled wonderful. New paintings, new statues, and new pedestals were arranged at pleasing intervals. She circled her new desk, half again the size of the previous one. It was old wood polished to a high sheen, the lighter accents in the natural grain again reminiscent of waves. She had barely settled in the expensive chair behind it— ergonomically perfect and made of a bulletproof weave— when her subordinate opened the door.

Danna Cudon had been with her since her first days in the gang. Usha had seen something in her at their initial meeting, a blend of determination and intensity that called to her. When the other woman had killed the leader of the Atlantean gang at her order without so much as flinching, she'd known they would be a team forever. The two killings that followed had cemented their bond. They were twin souls, one dark and the other darker, taking what they wanted from life. The woman seemed content to let her lead and never did a single thing to suggest she wanted the chair behind the desk.

Today, she was dressed in a charcoal pinstripe suit and shiny leather boots with laces peeking out from under her cuffs. Her tie was emerald over a black shirt. *A splash of color. She's happy today. I wonder what I missed.* A small smile spread over her lips. *Happy is good.* The men who entered behind her second did not look happy, however. The enforcers had arrived a few days before, and she had taken to using one of them as a bodyguard at all times. Their skills were far superior to standard muscle, however. They were a step down from New Atlantis' fighting elite, who were all directly in service to the Empress. The two would be motivated to serve, as a positive recommendation could earn them a place in the next contest for advancement to that select group.

They were negative twins with similar physiques and identical faces, one seemingly carved from dark stone and the other from light. Each sported a beard and mustache in Atlantean style, a mix of shaggy free portions and narrow braids, different enough from their skin tone to be noticeable. Tight black t-shirts, jeans, and boots were their standard uniform to allow freedom of movement and hide blood loss easily. It was impossible not to recognize them as members of the warrior culture that had bred them.

Danna spoke in a casual tone. "We are reporting as ordered, Ms Serris." That was for the benefit of the newcomers. They were never that formal one-on-one.

She nodded. "Thank you for coming. How are things?"

Her subordinate grinned. "Very good. All signs point in the right direction." There were no chairs except her own, so the other woman stopped across the desk to her right and the new additions stood side by side to her left.

Usha turned to regard them. "You have both done well so far."

They nodded in unison, and the dark one answered, "It is our honor to serve."

She leaned back and grinned. "But doubtless, you feel your talents are wasted watching over Ms Cudon and I. Speak freely."

The light man shrugged. "We are capable of much more, of course, but our purpose is to meet your needs. The nature of them doesn't matter."

"You see?" She turned her head to face Danna. "That's exactly how it should be. Ready, willing, and oh, so able." The flirty tone was intended only to tease her second. Easily caught prey lacked spice, and the obedient warriors would refuse her nothing, which made them uninteresting for anything other than work. *But for that, they'll be quite useful.*

She shifted to seriousness. "So. Report." Usha saw herself as an ideas person and as the force that was applied at pivotal moments to transform a situation. The day-to-day was handled by others under Danna's watchful eye.

Her second clasped her hands behind her back. Her pale skin was offset by the lush dark hair that fell straight to the middle of her back, and her cheekbones were sharp enough to cut. "We are expanding our presence in all the nightspots at the expected rate. The upper echelon has been difficult to penetrate, as you know, and many of those have required my personal attention."

A nod indicated her approval. "I will continue to assist you where needed. You have only to ask." She couldn't resist another tweak of her second, who disliked asking for help as much as she herself did.

Danna's small smile acknowledged the dig. "Our researchers have almost finalized the formula to use on the humans. It will be far more effective and addictive than any non-magical drug." The original plan had been also to make it fatal over time but first, Danna and then the Empress had counseled her against going so far, so fast. Her second had been concerned about putting the human gang in a corner prematurely while they were still strong enough to strike back. Her ruler had simply suggested that having a steady supply of workers would always be useful, all the more so when you were the sole source of what they desired.

"Excellent. That will provide us the funds we need

while weakening our enemies. What of the nuisances who broke in?"

"Almost certainly they are the two you believe them to be. Our watchers have seen them both at the tavern, together and separately. Of course, we cannot find out what's happening inside." Even though the rules would permit either group to spend time within the walls, there was an unspoken agreement to treat the establishment as sanctified ground for official meetings. The dwarf had been correct on that matter, at least. It was useful to know that if talking was required, there was an easy way to accomplish it. *Not that there'll ever be a need.*

"And the ill-advised attack on the girl?"

A barely perceptible wince flickered across Danna's face. Her second was the only person other than the Empress who Usha felt was as offended by unprofessional behavior as she was. "Those who were involved but not arrested have had their errors explained to them. Forcefully. What do you wish to do with those in jail?"

She shrugged. "Let them stay there for a while. This is a good time to build a channel into the prison system and find out who we can turn to our purposes. Threats, money, drugs, whatever." Danna was well-versed in all the possibilities. "If they try to relocate our people out of the area, though, we'll need to move."

The suited woman replied with a single nod. "Consider it done."

"So, what do you think we should do about Tanyith and the girl?" Asking questions for which she already had her own answers was a technique she had learned from the Empress.

"We should kill them, of course. Their transgression can only be answered by blood."

Usha nodded. "How?"

"I would be more than happy to do it myself."

"You are too valuable to risk on such menial tasks." Usha shook her head firmly. "Fortunately, the Empress has seen fit to grant us some assistance." She turned to face the men. "Which of you is the better fighter?"

Each replied simultaneously, "I am." It was what she'd expected.

"Which of you has more wins in the arena?"

The dark man smiled and revealed a mouth full of perfectly white pointed teeth. "I have one more."

His pale twin raised his chin. "Because we were dispatched on the day of my matching bout, which I doubtless would have won. But my brother is correct."

Usha nodded. "Then he shall have the honor of going first. Find the girl and kill her within the week. You will do this outside the hours when I require you as a bodyguard."

He inclined his head in acceptance. She waved the men to the door and beckoned for her second in command to join her on the couches. When they were gone, she asked, "So, do you think he'll succeed?"

Danna shrugged. "She has proven formidable so far, but I can only believe it's luck. There's no way she has the skills or experience to withstand an enforcer."

Usha shook her head. "It will be interesting to see. Her lineage requires us to tread more carefully than I'd prefer. If the Empress were to discover her before we have eliminated her like we did her parents, it would be a problem. Her guardians did a fine job hiding her from us. However, now that she's resurfaced, we must follow the rules appropriate to her station but move quickly enough to avoid notice from above."

Her second nodded. "Battles of increasing difficulty until she proves her worth or dies. Although you're starting her with a fairly hefty challenge."

"It is our way."

The other woman rose, sensing the dismissal in her tone. "Hers as well."

"Indeed. I wonder, do you think there's a chance we could turn her?"

Danna chuckled and shook her head. "Not a single one."

She sighed. "She might have been a useful puppet but you're right. She needs to die." She stood and returned to her desk as the other woman made her way out of the room. *Now to consider how best to remove the Tanyith-sized thorn in my side.*

CHAPTER SIX

R ion Grisham sat alone in his office and reflected upon the fact that he was not a happy man. His tenure as head of the Zatora Crime Syndicate was fresh enough that success was far from guaranteed, and each effort he made to lock down new territories or businesses seemed to be mired in tar. Between the Atlantean gang and the suddenly vocal minority magical communities in the Crescent City, every two steps forward were accompanied by at least one in the wrong direction.

At the same time, however, there was light at the end of this particular tunnel. By declaring themselves, his hidden enemies had become visible. The meeting at the tavern had trebled his suspicion that not all had been as it seemed with the break-in at the Zatora mansion. It was inconceivable that the culprits would try to fence the items so quickly. From there, it was a short jump to assume that someone else had been responsible, someone playing against both sides. Like the duo he'd met prior to the evening in question. *It's unfortunate Ozahl wasn't here on the night of the theft. He probably would have seen through their magic and we could have caught them in the act.*

The mage was paid enough that he didn't doubt his loyalty, especially since he'd pledged to outbid any other offer the man received. He was the leader's secret ace in the hole, as the organization's public image made the idea of hiring magicals or accepting them into the group inconceivable. Occasionally, he worried that word might get out, but there were plans in place for that eventuality. Other plans were ready should the wizard try to betray him. Overall, it was an arrangement that, so far, had worked well and promised to do so into the future.

He rose from the couch and turned toward the door at a vibration on his wrist. His people had been ordered not to bother him until the wizard returned, so he didn't have to look to know that the event had occurred. He rolled the sleeves of his button-down shirt to his elbows as he walked toward the hidden room in the basement which the intruders had missed during their theft. A guard stood outside the door, and he gave him a nod as he brushed past. Inside, a man thrashed in a reclining metal chair that would have seemed more appropriate in a dentist's office, his wrists and ankles shackled to the furniture. A cloth gag prevented speech, but there were shouts behind it.

The wizard stood nearby and gazed silently at the prisoner. He looked different again today—thinner and with a beard and short hair. Rion had demanded a way to always know it was him, so he had presented him with a ring that cooled whenever he was nearby. "Evening, my friend. What have you brought me?" He'd asked for several things

—four, to be exact. The intruders and his own freelancing gang members.

"This is one of the men who broke in according to the camera footage from the hallway and upstairs." There were no recording devices in his office, of course. "An acquaintance of mine saw him in a bar in Dallas, of all places, and was kind enough to give him up. For a fee, naturally."

Rion nodded. "We'll make it good. Has he said anything?"

"Nothing useful. Some protests and some screams, that's all. He didn't come quietly, even though I asked him to politely."

"Imagine that." He approached the bound man. "So you thought you'd steal from me, huh? Well, we'll settle that score before the night is out. But first, how about you tell me everything you know about the Atlantean gang, working backward from why you broke in here."

He nodded and the mage gestured. The knot in the gag untied itself and it levitated away. The prisoner coughed and took a few moments to simply breathe. He had long braids and dark eyes and was dressed in ratty jeans and a rattier t-shirt. Finally, he collected himself enough to look up. "I didn't do it."

He sighed. "You showed him the video, right?"

"Of course," Ozhal's said beside him.

"So, I'll ask you again. Why?"

Their captive looked close to tears. "I'm telling you, it wasn't me. I was already at the police station when it happened."

Rion frowned. "It looks like you." He turned to the mage. "It does, right? Look like him?"

"It does indeed."

He turned back in feigned confusion. "See, it looks like you. How can it not be you? This is your last chance to say something useful before I break a bone or two."

The prisoner's words tumbled out in a panic. "It wasn't me. The witch detective—Baron or whatever—picked me and my buddy up on the street. She showed us pictures of us doing things we didn't do and told us to get out of town. It was a frame-up. I'm telling you it wasn't me." The last word changed into a shriek as the mage did something to him.

The gang leader turned to his employee. "Now, now, let the man speak. You can play later." One more gesture drew another squeal before Ozhal nodded. Rion regarded the soon-to-be-broken man in the chair. "Okay, let's say I believe you. What will you give me so I convince my friend here not to spend an entire day breaking pieces off you?"

"I don't have much of anything." The man gulped. "The policewoman wanted to hear all about the gang and what we're doing. But I'm a street soldier, man, and only ran a little protection. I've heard rumors but I don't know anything." There was an unmistakable plea in his voice for acceptance or mercy or some other thing he wouldn't receive.

"Tell me the rumors, then."

"Drugs. Special merchandise for people from Oriceran and not for humans. Lining up businesses to pay tribute. Some folks coming off the boat owing the gang money. That kind of thing."

Rion glanced at the wizard, who responded with a noncommittal shrug. *Some help you are. I need a mind reader or a truth-teller or something. Heh. Someone who can see the future would be nice. But I suppose if the magic aliens had one of those, I'd already have lost.* "Do you have anything else useful to share?"

"No, man, I've told you everything. The detective said to get out of town before my own side came after me, so I did. That's all."

He nodded and motioned for the mage to follow him into the hallway. The gag flew into place over the man's mouth and drew renewed screams from him. Once outside, he asked, "So, my read is that the detective was working with the dwarf's people on this if she knew to scoop him up ahead of time. It's probably the same with my guys."

"Illusions, almost certainly. It explains a lot."

"Did they really think we'd be dumb enough to fall for it?"

The other man shrugged. "Maybe, maybe not. It could be that they didn't believe it would hold but simply needed to throw us off the scent for a short time. They haven't shown themselves to be stupid yet, so I assume they expected we'd see through it before too long."

"That group is a problem."

Ozahl nodded. "But your plan to bide your time is a good one. Eventually, we'll find a way to separate some from the rest or to strike directly at the ones who dared to break in here."

"It's the two we picked up at the club."

"Very likely. But that doesn't change anything. If we have the chance, sure, we kill them. But there's no point in facing all the magicals at once, which would probably be the result. No, we need to do it in a way that gives us deni-ability."

Rion clapped him on the shoulder. "I'll think about that. Enjoy yourself, but how about some soundproofing, huh?" The mage grinned, nodded, and entered the room again. The prisoner's shrieks quickly went silent. He wandered back to his office, thinking hard. *There has to be a way to get at those two and blame it on the Atlanteans. I merely have to find it.*

CHAPTER SEVEN

After he'd noticed Fyre lurking outside the week before, Sensei Ikehara had insisted that the Draksa —who he saw as a dark brown Rottweiler—join them in the dojo. He wasn't allowed on the mat, naturally, but was permitted in the front of the studio before it opened. Cali hadn't minded at first, but as her teacher threw her effortlessly to the canvas for the seventh or eighth time in a row, she was sure the little beast was laughing at her.

Of course, the assumption that Fyre found his amusement at her expense was usually fairly reliable. She scrambled to her feet, ignored the ache in her muscles, and regarded the man across from her. He was dressed in a white uniform top secured by a black belt over a hakama in the same shade. The dark scruff that always shadowed his face and upper lip was slightly thicker than usual, and his dark eyes watched her carefully. His voice was gruff and focused, as it often was during their one-on-one training sessions. "Again. This time, try to keep yourself upright."

She groaned and moved in again, trying to anticipate his reaction so she could use it against him. When she shifted to her left and thrust her right hand out in a feint, he flowed smoothly out of the way. His palm grasped her wrist, but she twisted to avoid his lock and scuttled to the right. He pursued—another change from the group classes where a single escape was usually instructionally adequate —and attempted to put her in a chokehold. She met it with force, an inappropriate block in Aikido, but it opened him for a kick.

Cali snapped her leg forward and the idea that she would finally connect with one of her attacks brought a wide grin to her face. The realization that it was a setup struck her a moment before he slipped to the right and locked his arms on her shoulder, then used the leverage to push her to the mat over his extended leg. As her spine struck the canvas surface, she was sure she heard a snort from the front of the room.

With a sigh, she pushed herself to her feet once more. Ikehara grinned. "Again."

Once the sparring had reached the point where her teacher apparently felt she'd suffered enough, they changed to weapons. He'd demanded that she use her magical sticks so she could continue to improve her feel for them, and she'd happily obliged. In previous sessions, he had attacked her with his own sticks, a wooden bokken, and both a bo and a jo staff. Today, he two-handed the sword. It sliced at her from above, and she raised her weapons in an X to catch it, then guided it to the side with a spin.

Her stick whistled toward his head, and he barely managed to get the block up in time. She doubled down and launched successive blows he struggled to intercept with the larger weapon. Her nimbleness gave her an advantage, and she pressed forward. Finally, he stumbled unexpectedly and provided an opening. She stabbed forward and tapped him lightly on the temple.

A surge of pleasure washed through her at her success, banished instantly by his belligerent response. "No. If you continue to behave this way, we will have to end your training."

Her hands lowered in shock. "What?" The fact that she'd forgotten to use his title or show any other form of respect was a clear indication of her surprise.

He gestured with the sword. "You had me. Why did you stop?"

"What?" Her confusion was complete.

Ikehara signaled for her to kneel, lowered himself to his knees opposite her, and placed the bokken carefully beside him. "You have developed a fear and are afraid to hurt me. On the one hand, this is good because you acknowledge your own power and abilities." He raised a palm. "On the other, it caused you to practice in an unrealistic fashion."

"So, you're saying I should have struck you with my full strength?"

He nodded. "If you do not trust me to take care of myself, how can we train together? If you fail to trust your partners, how can you fight together?"

Fyre snorted again from the front of the room, clearly in agreement with her instructor. She shook her head. "I don't want to hurt you."

He shrugged. "That is a risk we must both accept for you to reach your highest potential. But it seems as if this may be a bigger question for you than our sparring would suggest."

Cali looked at the mat and let her hair fall in front of her face. She disliked all the thoughts that ran through her head and the remembered snatches of dreams where she was forced to hurt her friends that surfaced in her mind. She didn't want to answer but knew he wouldn't let her off the hook. None of the people she cared for ever did. "I'm more powerful than I was. I'm dangerous."

His voice was calm and inquisitive—the "teacher's" tone he used in class with new students. "Every person who gets behind the wheel of a car is dangerous. What makes you different?"

She shrugged. "I'm training to hurt people. On purpose, not like a car accident."

"So you're dangerous and working to increase your abilities. That will give you more control as well as more ability to do damage. It seems as if those are in balance."

"Who am I to decide?" she asked and sighed.

He chuckled. "You are you, Caliste. You are a born warrior. A crusader. A champion. This is clear to all who know you if it is not yet obvious to you."

She blinked, unable to fathom his meaning. *Me? Some kind of hero? I can barely get my homework done on time.* Her body trembled and she fought to still it. *Don't freak out, Cali. Settle down.* She pushed out the words stuck in her throat and they emerged in a whisper. "I make mistakes—so many mistakes. Now, they might hurt people and maybe even kill them."

The tip of the bokken tapped her chin as Ikehara forced her to raise her head. She mustered her will and met his gaze. "So. To quote one of the most important texts of the last hundred years, 'with great power comes great responsibility.' You cannot give up the power so you must accept the responsibility."

"Do you think I'm strong enough?" She vehemently disliked the part of her that craved his reassurance but pushed that worry aside.

Ikehara gave a sharp nod. "I do. But only if you fully accept yourself." A small smile appeared at the corner of his mouth. "Mistakes and all."

His words filled the hole inside her that had slowly expanded throughout their training session. She answered his nod with one of her own. "Okay. I don't have any idea how to do that."

He laughed, a joyful sound in the seriousness of the moment. "Knowing your own ignorance is the first step toward enlightenment."

She chuckled. "More Spiderman?"

His smile fully materialized. "Patrick Rothfuss. Have you read him?"

"No." She rolled her eyes.

He rose smoothly to his full height. "You should. He has much to say but needs to write faster, though."

Cali stood. "All right, I think I'm ready."

Her instructor took several steps back and raised his blade in a defensive posture. "Then hit me if you can."

She surged into the attack, intent on making his order a reality.

The session sufficiently exhausted Cali that she fell asleep the moment they returned to the apartment. As soon as she was resting deeply enough not to notice, Fyre climbed to his feet from where he lay on the rug beside her bed. The conversation they'd had earlier had left him uncomfortable and reminded him of something he simply couldn't remember.

He felt confined, cooped up, and like a part of him was missing. The apartment was too small. He padded to the window and nudged it open with his magic. A simple veil protected him from sight as he launched himself into the air. He spread his wings wider than he had in a week, caught the breeze, and pushed himself upward with strong strokes. As he climbed higher and higher, he spiraled to catch a full view of the city. From above, it was a collection of shapes rather than structures, and the blue river called to him.

The Draksa flew to it, dove, and flashed into the water with a giant splash. His wings were as effective underwater as above, and he glided gracefully along the bottom, disturbing the silt as he passed. He summoned a shield above him to keep it from rising to betray his position. All his kind breathed in water as easily as in air—part of their innate magical nature—and were completely at home beneath the surface. He coasted to a stop and settled into the cool alluvium. The quiet allowed him to think.

He had no regrets over his choice of partner. Cali was definitely his kind of human. He wasn't sure why that was, but he was happy it was. Maybe it was instinct. Lately, he'd wished his memory was clearer and that he had more than only urges to lead him. Fortunately, he was adaptable and didn't spend too much time fretting. *It would be nice to remember more, though.*

Two fish whipped past overhead, and he entertained the idea of chasing and eating them for a moment. An odd sound distracted him, and he spent several seconds trying to discern what it might have been before it was warped by distance and waves. *A scream, maybe. Or a shout, but not a happy one.*

Fyre pushed up with his powerful legs and whipped his wings to gain speed. Sunlight greeted him as he broke the surface with water trailing from his body. He called in his veil again as he curved in the direction the sound had most likely come from. There were large buildings on the opposite shore, and he focused on them. Another sound surged through the air, definitely a scream this time. He turned toward it and headed to an abandoned-looking warehouse. When he reached it, he pulled up short and hovered in place with strong sweeps of his wings to peer through the broken places in the dirty windows.

Inside, a group of four men in jeans and matching leather vests over t-shirts stood in a loose circle around a fifth, who clambered slowly off the floor. His face was bloody and he whimpered as he moved. As soon as he gained his feet, one of the men darted in and punched him in the nose to fell him again with another scream.

Fyre growled quietly. While some three-on-one battles

might be fair, this one clearly was not. Still, he waited, not sure what was going on. Perhaps these humans were playing a strange game? He couldn't recall seeing anything like it but with his spotty memory, he wasn't positive.

The man on the far left—bald-headed, muscular, and sporting a chain that hung down the right-hand side of his dirty jeans—dispelled his concerns. "Well, now, Jimmy, it's too bad you decided to open your mouth to the wrong people. We can't have that."

The man on the ground shook his head and spoke fast. "No, I didn't. The police sweated me but I didn't say nothin'. I wouldn't say nothin' never."

His accuser knelt to meet his gaze. "We all know you have no spine, Jimmy. Lying is all you're good for. And now that we've had our fun, it's time for you to go bye-bye."

The speaker rose and drew a gun from behind his back. Fyre launched himself forward and shattered the glass panes as he entered, already breathing frost at the man with the weapon. The cone caught the one nearest him as well and froze them both in place. He dropped the veil so the remaining man and his intended victim could see him, and both yelled and retreated to the far corner of the room.

The remaining attacker produced a gun from somewhere and managed to squeeze off an impotent round before Fyre's tail whipped in a vicious ark and broke his hand. He whimpered and cradled it. The Draksa shook his head slowly. Since Cali wasn't with him and no one had seen him with her in his true form, there was no need to keep his abilities secret. He hissed, "Tell me who you are. Jimmy first."

The brown-haired and bearded man was wide-eyed and stammering. "Jimmy. I'm Jimmy."

Sigh. Fyre managed not to roll his eyes and instead, produced a threatening growl. "We've covered that. Tell me more."

"Uh, I'm with this gang. These guys. The Coypus."

The stupidity here is overwhelming. "Your group is named after giant rodents?"

"Yeah, 'cause we're everywhere, you know?"

"What I know is that you all clearly share only a single ill-working brain among you." He turned to regard the other man. "If you wish to avoid finding yourself frozen like your friends, now would be a good time to add something useful to the conversation."

The man whimpered and shook his head. Jimmy blurted, "He's Johnny. We were a team once. Jimmy and Johnny. But I messed up, I guess. I got caught. Now, I'm out." He turned to the other man with a question on his face and received a nod. "Yeah, I'm out. The new boss doesn't give second chances."

"What happened to the old boss?"

The man laughed. "He's dead. He tried to refuse the Zatoras and it didn't work out for him. The rest of us didn't care. As long as the money flows, it's all good." He frowned suddenly and turned to the other man. "Until it's not. You were going to help them kill me!" Fyre blasted them both with ice to cover them and lock them in place before Jimmy's punch could reach the head of his former friend.

The Draksa sighed and spoke to the room full of statues. "This is when I could really use fingers. And one of those phones everyone carries." He moved to a position outside the sightlines of the frozen gangmembers and cast a portal to take him to Cali's room. Fortunately, she had both fingers and a phone. *Now, I simply have to find a way to wake her without getting attacked.*

CHAPTER EIGHT

At a loud crash, Cali whirled on the four Kilomea in the back corner of the tavern. "That's the third one so far. Quit breaking things." One of them looked sheepish and held the pieces of a stew bowl in his hands. She shook her head and stormed over to them. "Listen. You all need to either accept that you have to use wooden or metal bowls or start paying for the ones you break. Make a damn choice."

The giant she liked best, who had a wide face and soft eyes to balance his oversized muscular body, laughed in his unnaturally deep voice. "Little one, we apologize. You know that each new person we bring with us has to learn on their own. It's part of the fun."

She shook her head again. "I feel like Zeb will back me up on this. Any breakage now gets added to your tab. We're not made of bowls here." She looked at the floor but apparently, the bowl had been empty when it was broken. *Thank heavens for small favors.* She kicked a tiny shard into the corner where she'd almost certainly forget to retrieve it later and moved on the next demanding customer.

When she returned to the bar several minutes later with a tray of empties in her hand, Zeb chuckled at her. "You know I don't care about the broken bowls, right?"

She grinned as she put the glasses on the bar for him to wash. "I know. But they're so big, they don't get messed with enough. I feel it's my responsibility."

He laughed outright. "Have you checked on the beastie lately?"

Cali shook her head. "No, I'll go take a look now if you can handle the place."

Zeb gave her a glare in response and she wandered off to the basement. When she'd left him, Fyre had been snoring on one of the crates, laying on his back like a fat cat. Now, he was curled up tail to nose like a less fat but still equally exhausted feline. She bopped him gently on the nose. "Hey, partner, are you all right?"

An eyelid opened to reveal a slitted pupil. "Yes." He uncurled and stretched, hopped to the ground, and shimmered as he adopted his Rottweiler illusion. "I simply didn't think it would look right if I wandered up there without you."

"Good call. Everyone knows you're very smart for a dog, but that might be pushing it." She led him up the stairs and detoured into the dining room as he ambled behind the bar. Zeb disappeared from view, presumably to give the Draksa some welcoming pets and scratches. The two had become almost inseparable when they were in proximity, a situation that made her heart happy.

As if her positive moment needed balancing, fate

brought someone to the entrance who guaranteed that the good vibes wouldn't last for long. Detective Kendra Barton strode inside, careful not to slam the door, and walked to the bar to trade verbal sallies with Zeb. His face displayed wary respect, so Cali wasn't able to dislike her too much, but the dark-haired woman's appearances rarely resulted in anything being easier. The way the detective's eyes tracked her as she delivered drinks and picked up empties suggested that today wouldn't be any different.

She lingered a little longer in the common area than strictly necessary but finally had no excuses left and made her way to the front of the room. Barton's small grin showed she was aware of the deliberate delay. "Cali." The woman's voice was neutral and professional.

Deliberately, she infused fake joy into her own. "Kendra, how lovely to see you. Can I find you a seat? Perhaps among the Kilomea in the corner?" She'd love to discover how long the representative of the New Orleans Police Department would last under the challenging provocations of the martial-minded giants.

Barton shook her head. "No, I'm good. I only came to chat. Do you have a minute?"

Cali fake-cringed. "Oh, geez, now isn't a great time." She gestured at the customers. "I'm really busy and they're rowdy tonight, and my boss will get mad. Maybe come back in a week or two?"

The detective rolled her eyes and Zeb chuckled. "Be nice, Cali. Technically, she's a customer, too." He handed her a soda with lime, the only thing the woman had ever accepted in the tavern, then turned the bar gun and sprayed a stream of liquid out of sight. She heard Fyre's mouth snap at it and had to laugh.

"Okay, sure. What do you need?"

"I had a weird gang incident crop up on the other side of the river. We had a random call on the tip line from an unlisted number. Anyway, the one person we managed to track from the location and bring in said something about a dragon. I decided this would be the place to ask about it. Do you know anything?"

It took effort but she managed to keep her expression neutral. "I've never seen a dragon except on the sign." *That's technically true. Fyre is a Draksa, not a dragon. And there's no way to trace that call back to me.* "Hopefully, you don't think one of them came to life or something? Because that would be weird."

Kendra shook her head. "No, surely not that. But it's like this tavern is the epicenter for weirdness of late. Do you know there are usually people watching the place?"

Zeb chuckled. "Other than your people, you mean, Detective?"

Barton nodded. "Exactly. Several others."

The dwarf shrugged. "We can't control what others do. As long as they follow the rules while they're inside and don't mess with our customers when they arrive or leave, they're welcome to waste their time staring at the door." He turned to Cali with a grin. "Perhaps we should start an outdoor service? Offer them food and drink?"

She shook her head. "I have more than enough to do, thanks. Maybe you could handle that part yourself."

The detective looked off to the side for an instant before she turned to the door. It opened to reveal Tanyith, who Cali hadn't seen for a few days. *Clearly, she's in contact with her people on the outside. It makes sense.* Her partner in crime was dressed for a night out in a fashionable suit and tie. *He cleans up nice.* She watched Barton notice him and saw the small grin she tried to hide. *Uh-huh. There's something there. I'm not sure what, but something.*

He looked from the detective to Zeb and then to her, and smiled in confusion. "Did I miss a meeting invitation? Or are you planning a surprise party for me? Really, you shouldn't have."

Barton gave him her detective's stare. "What, are your gang buddies not taking care of you, Shalen?" Cali blinked and realized that she'd never actually heard his surname.

He laughed. "Good detecting. You've cracked the case of my last name. So you don't have to spend any more time, my nickname used to be Shale. I've left both names behind, exactly like the Atlantean gang. Now, I'm only Tanyith, except on my driver's license."

Cali sighed loudly. "It's shameless the way you flirt with him, Kendra. Maybe you two should find a room so you can get it out of your system. Not here, of course," she hurried to add. She turned her head to look at Zeb. "I won't be able to go into the back rooms tonight because of the image that I just had. Or, maybe, ever." She made a theatrical shudder.

The other woman put her head in her palm for a minute, then looked up with a sigh. "It is really difficult to do nice things for you people. But a deal is a deal. The ship I gave you the info on has been rescheduled—something about a hurricane, apparently. It'll be in a week from Wednesday."

Tanyith frowned. "You're not messing with us, I hope."

She shook her head. "I keep my promises, Shalen. All of them. You'd both be wise to remember that." She waved at Zeb and turned to the door. No one stopped her and soon, she was out of sight.

"Wait one," Cali said and made a circuit through the customers to ensure that everyone was taken care of. There were drinks to deliver, empties and bowls to clean up, and tabs to collect, and it was almost a half-hour before she was caught up enough to rejoin the men. They were laughing together and Tanyith sipped something out of one of the small glasses Zeb reserved for his cask specials, which were usually fairly potent. *Sips are an appropriate choice. You continue to be smarter than you look.*

The dwarf nodded at her arrival. "Good timing. We were talking about you."

She frowned. "What about me?"

"That you're probably in danger," Tanyith replied.

She laughed. "Yeah, the ambush kind of gave that one away, genius. Very helpful. Thanks for stopping by. You can go now."

He gave Zeb a look that she read as exasperation and swiveled to face her directly. "No, I mean bigger danger than that. Our little game with the disguises would never have held for long, and the fact that you've had eyes on you in multiple places is telling. The ambush was minor league. I'm honestly surprised they tried it."

"It didn't feel minor when the fire tried to cook me."

"Okay, minor league zealots," he said with a shrug. "But still not the way either of the gang leaders would have done it. They'd want it to be personal and drawn out. It kind of has to be to answer for our offense."

She sighed. *Yeah, I know, but it's not like there's much we can do about it.* "What about you? Do you think they're targeting both of us?"

"I'm less predictable than you are. I move around constantly and I don't have a job to go to yet, so they probably can't get a solid bead on me. But with you, they know if they watch the square, the tavern, and your dojo, you're bound to appear at one of them on any given day."

She set the tray she'd forgotten she was holding on the bar and climbed onto the seat beside him. Fortunately, the elderly wizards who often held down several chairs across from Zeb and made enough noise for three times their number were absent that evening. "Do you think that my friends or Emalia are in danger?"

Zeb nodded, a serious look on his face. "More than they would be if they had no connection to you, to be sure. You should warn them to skedaddle if they have any suspicions about a person or a situation."

"Skedaddle? Really?" She shook her head. "Honestly, it's like you get a year older with every passing month. I thought dwarves were supposed to live longer, not get prematurely senile."

His tone was amused. "Valerie wouldn't like to hear you talk that way."

She looked at his battle ax prominently displayed above the bar. It was a visible threat but never more than that. She'd never seen him hold it in anger and frankly, had a difficult time imagining that he ever had. He merely didn't seem the type. "Yeah. You'll hit me with an ax for being a smart-mouth. Sure, Zeb."

Tanyith laughed. "She's got you there. You need to cultivate a scarier persona, clearly. Outside these walls, the stories are ominous, but once someone meets you, they kind of fray around the edges."

In another life, Zeb must have been a monk given how disconnected he seemed from minor—or major—worries. He simply grinned and nodded. "That's the way I like it. Mysterious."

Cali rapped her knuckles on the bar. "Anyway, back to the exceedingly important topic at hand. My safety." She paused to collect her thoughts. "I'm of the opinion that the best defense is to strike them while they're still thinking about attacking you."

Tanyith shrugged. "Scale is an issue. There's a large number of them and only two of us. Three if you count Zeb."

"Four if you count Fyre, but yeah, I see the problem." She exhaled a low sigh. "We'll simply have to let it lie for now and see how it turns out. I'll keep my eyes open."

"Me too." Her partner turned to the dwarf. "Maybe you can have a chat with the people you know and have them watch for trouble too?"

He nodded. "They're already on it. Everyone's doing what they can because no one wants to see this situation escalate."

Cali shook her head. "No one but the Zatoras and the Atlanteans, anyway. I don't think it'll end while they're both still around."

Tanyith raised his glass, took a large sip, and impressively managed to avoid coughing. "Knowing the Atlanteans like I do, I'd say that's a very fair assessment." He lifted his drink in a toast. "To teamwork and staying alive, then." A deep gulp finished it and he stood only slightly unsteadily. "Now, I need to get home. I have an appointment tomorrow."

She made a woo-ing sound. "Hot date?"

He gave one of the softest smiles she'd ever seen on his face. "An old friend."

"Old female friend."

Rather than reply, he merely turned and wandered out the door. Once it closed behind him, she leaned closer to Zeb and whispered, "You know what, I bet she's not old at all."

The dwarf laughed. "No, not with that look on his face. Doubtless, she's more age-appropriate than some."

Cali scowled. "Don't you start. And don't tell me you don't see the sparks from Barton when he's around, either. She's the one he needs to watch out for. It's never good to consort with the enemy."

He gave one last chuckle. "She's closer to friend than foe. Jealous much?"

She gave him a pitying shake of her head. "Stop trying to use young-people lingo, Zeb. It only makes you look sad." With a wink, she snatched her tray up and returned to the customers.

CHAPTER NINE

Tanyith strode up the sidewalk to Sienna's house with flowers clutched in his left hand. This time, he'd purchased them from a street vendor rather than picking at random from the garden islands decorating the lane. He was fairly sure the points he'd lose for off-the-cuff thoughtfulness would be regained for not destroying her neighborhood.

Unlike the first occasion, when he'd arrived unannounced and saturated with trepidation, he had been invited this time. Despite her parting words a week and a half or so earlier, he hadn't really expected her to be receptive to another visit. The fact that she'd been the one to reach out filled him with positive vibes. *Don't get too crazy here, Tanyith. It's a long way from having a drink together to rekindling a flame that might have burned all the way out for her.*

The door opened without him having to knock, and the sight of her took his breath away, exactly as it always had. Her eyes were a beautiful trap, sparkling, intense, and deep enough to fall into. All that surrounded them was gorgeous, but he'd constantly been captured first by those luminous pools. That much, at least, hadn't changed.

He stopped on the porch and grinned, probably like a fool. "Hi, See."

She smiled. "Hi yourself." She reached out for the flowers, took them, and sniffed deeply. "Beautiful. Come on in."

With a laugh, he stepped through the doorway behind her. "Thanks for the compliment."

She groaned. "Stupid joke, stupid person."

Exactly like old times. "The joke isn't bad merely because the audience is too unsophisticated for it."

She walked into the kitchen and pulled a vase down from a cabinet. "Yeah, sophistication. That's the issue." She twisted the handle to run water into the vessel, then turned to set it on the island between them. Her long fingers retrieved a small knife from the drawer and she twirled it once like a performer before she sliced the stems at an angle and dropped the bouquet in the vase. "Seriously, though, the flowers are very pretty. You were thoughtful to bring them."

Her tone, suddenly less playful, warned him she had something on her mind. "What's up, Sienna?"

She shook her head. "Drink first. I want to know what you've been up to."

Again, it was like it always had been. Despite being a free spirit, certain formalities existed in her world that must be observed. Chief among them was her desire to be a good host. He followed her to the living room, where a set of four glasses stood around an ice bucket and a bottle of amber liquid. She sat cross-legged on one battered couch and gestured him to the nearby matching chair, then used metal tongs to plink cubes into two tumblers and poured. "Infused ginger bourbon."

He took the glass, sipped, and nodded in appreciation as the whiskey burned its way across his tongue and into his throat. "Delicious. You have always been a genius when it comes to flavors."

Sienna raised an eyebrow. "Not only that."

Tanyith laughed. "Indeed. Not only. So, let's have it."

She frowned. "It feels weird asking you to do this for me."

He shrugged. "We have too much shared history to worry about that kind of stuff, and you know it. Hit me."

Her sigh spoke volumes. "After we broke up, I dated a guy for a while. I really liked him. Things were going well, I thought, and then he flat-out vanished. Gone like he'd never existed. Numbers didn't work, and he wasn't around any of the places where he had been." She frowned and studied her hands, which were folded in her lap. "I'm kind of ashamed to say I looked for him. Hard. I was a little crazy."

The confession unsettled him but he laughed. "Been there. Sometimes, the brain winds up stuck in a loop it can't get out of." He knew the guy she was talking about because while he hadn't neared stalker status, he had spent more hours than were healthy in the nightspots she frequented after they'd split. The sight of them together had been like lava in his belly. "It gets better. It merely takes time."

"It's been almost a year and I'm still not past it. So...I know you must need work and I have some money set aside. I'll hire you to look into his disappearance. We could do a contract or whatever you want and we both win. You make some cash and I get some closure."

He shook his head. "I'll do it for free."

"No. Just…no." Pain or guilt or both flickered across her face. "This can only work if I pay you. That's the only way I won't feel dirty about it. Please, say you'll do it."

Unsure how she would take his next question, he hesitated. "What if the news is bad?"

She sniffed and made kind of a half-laugh and half-sob. "It can't be worse than the answers my brain gives me." She raised her eyes to meet his. "It's not about the romance anymore. I don't think there's anything that could bridge the gap. I simply need to know why. Was it me? Was it something else? It chews on me."

"And if I find him and he won't answer?"

Sienna raised her hands, then let them drop. "That would be something, anyway. I can work with that but I can't handle the absence of some kind of explanation."

Tanyith nodded. "Needing resolution is something I understand well. I had thirteen months to think about nothing else."

She managed a half-smile. "So you'll do it, then?"

"I will. Let's call it twenty-five an hour plus expenses. Does that sound good?"

"You could go higher."

He shook his head. "I'm not exactly in demand at the moment and it's not like I have a mortgage or anything. Plus, this gives me the flexibility to keep working on my own stuff at the same time. Win-win."

"Win-win," Sienna echoed.

"But there's one catch."

She chuckled. "There always was, with you. What is it?"

"You have to let me take you out to dinner."

"Are you sure that's a good idea?"

"There's no way to tell until we do it. No pressure, only dinner. With dancing as your exclusive option."

"It's lonely in prison, huh?" She raised an eyebrow.

When he broke into laughter, she joined him. After a moment, he was able to speak again and said, "Yes, it was, but that's not the reason. It was circumstances that pulled us apart before. Now, those have changed. Maybe there could be something more than friendship for us. If not, we'd still have a nice meal together. But I'd like to be sure. You know, for the sake of closure."

She shook her head. "Well played, Tay."

"Is that a yes?"

Sienna nodded. "It is. I'm busy this weekend. A week from Friday?"

"Deal. Now, do you have any idea where I should start looking for this person who was stupid enough to leave you?"

"Yeah. But you definitely won't like the answer."

"I hear that often lately. Tell me anyway."

"He was hanging around the Horsehead mostly toward the end."

He muttered a curse under his breath. "Any other leads?"

She shook her head. "No, that's it. I told you it wouldn't make you happy." He rose and she matched his movement and wrapped him in a hug. She whispered, "Thank you."

For a moment, he rested his chin on her head. "You got

it, See. I always said you were irresistible. It seems like it's still true." She laughed into his chest and there were more words, but his brain had already moved on to the next task. When the door closed behind him, he pulled his phone out and pressed the second speed dial button.

Moments later, a brusque voice answered. "Barton. Who's this?"

"Tanyith."

She barked a short laugh. "How'd you get this number, Shale?"

He sighed inwardly and chose not to give her the pleasure of rising to the bait and correcting her again. "It's nice to have friends, Detective. So, I thought in the interest of continuing our partnership on good terms, you might be willing to answer a question for me."

She replied neutrally, "First, let me clarify that I owe you exactly nothing. But go ahead and ask."

"What do you know about the Stallion Bar?"

A note of interest entered her tone. "A lot, actually. Why are you asking?"

"A friend requested that I look into someone who disappeared. He was last seen hanging out there."

"Recently?"

"Nah. Long gone, but that's all I have to go on."

"So you're a private eye now?"

He laughed. "Are you gonna keep breaking my balls, Detective? I have other people I can approach for information."

A smile crept into her voice. "Nah, I'll give you this one for free. It's a gathering place for the human gangs in town, usually but not always peacefully."

That confirmed his perception of it. His friends had taken to calling it the Horsehead because of the scene from *The Godfather.* "So that's one more thing that hasn't changed since my time."

"You probably won't be particularly welcome there, given your history."

"I doubt anyone there will know me anymore."

"It depends. It's run by the Zatoras now. Is there any reason they might recognize you?"

He winced. *Not good.* "Nothing more than any other guy, I suppose, Detective."

"Uh-huh. I'm not stupid, Shale. If you decide to leave neutral territory, be careful, okay? I'd hate to have to explain to Caliste how the guy who's been hitting on her died suddenly and violently."

Somehow, he managed not to growl. "I'm not hitting on her."

"Sure, sure." He wasn't able to read her voice, but he sensed that she was playing with him. "So, anything else, Philip Marlowe?"

Again, he couldn't help but laugh. "No thanks, Columbo, I'm set."

"See you around. Try to make sure it's not on a slab, okay?"

"I'll do my best, Detective. Same to you."

She clicked off without responding, and he shook his head. *Kendra Barton is the most annoying woman I've ever met. But damn, she's good.*

CHAPTER TEN

So many things had changed in Cali's life since the death of her parents, but this room in the back of Emalia's place remained constant with the same beat-up table, the same vinyl-covered chairs, and the same chipped tea set. It provided constant reassurance that the world would keep turning and that she could always depend upon it and upon her former guardian, ongoing mentor, and only known relative to remain steadfast.

Her aunt had decided to keep her shop closed today and was in what Cali thought of as her "loungewear"—a grey Loyola sweatsuit and large fuzzy slippers. It was far from a regular look for the woman but it suited her. At their feet, Fyre lay curled in his natural form to take up as little space as possible in the cramped room. She had offered to share a bigger place with the other woman, but the answer was always the same. "I have what I need and that is sufficient."

I have what I need too. But I'm not sure I have enough space for the lummox at my feet. Especially if he grows any larger.

The jury was still out on whether Fyre would grow beyond his current size, but the possibility couldn't be discounted. Emalia poured tea into both cups, a new brew she'd said she was testing to see if it was more energizing than the last one. She sipped it with a grimace, and the older woman laughed.

"You kids today can't handle a little bitterness."

"This isn't merely bitter. This is like licking the pure essence of bitterness. You may have cracked a hole in the entire bitterness-space-time continuum with this creation." She took another sip. "Okay, it gets slightly better. Now, it's only horrible rather than deadly."

"Wimp."

She laughed. "Woo, tough words. Are you sure you want to break out the big guns on your grandniece like that?"

Emalia rolled her eyes. "Impudent whelp." She couldn't keep the edges of her mouth from twitching up, though.

"If you dislike the monster you created, that's on you, Doctor Frankenstein."

The older woman shook her head. "You spend too much time on the streets with your friends. It's made your tongue sharp. Where's the respect for your elders?"

Cali stared incredulously at her until they both broke into laughter. "You've taught me everything I know, lady. You have only yourself to blame."

Her aunt nodded and feigned sadness. "It's a pity. I have no idea where I went wrong."

The banter subsided into a comfortable silence until the tea was finished and her teacher tilted her chin at her. "So, what do you wish to practice today?"

She scratched the back of her neck. "I'm not sure. I have to work on maintaining my disguises better, but that's not new. Things are getting a little scarier out there, though, and I feel like I might need to be much stronger and faster in order to deal with it. So, can you make that happen?"

The older woman released a soft laugh and shook her head. "If only it worked that way, my child. But it doesn't. Magical skill, like any skill, is only learned through practice and more practice."

"So, what would you recommend? I've faced force, fire, shadow, and lightning. Oh, and ice from this doofus." She gave Fyre a gentle kick, and he snorted chill fog up the leg of her jeans, which made her shudder.

Emalia shrugged. "Any and all of them would be useful for fighting enemies directly. As time permits, you should test each one. But it seems as if you might be best served to avoid direct opposition when you can—evade a strike more than meet force with force to block it. True?"

Cali nodded. "Sensei Ikehara would say that is the best way. Who am I to argue? Besides, I have Fyre to handle the direct stuff." She laughed. "Although my Aikido teacher—and everyone else who really knows me—would also point out that I go with force against force as a default."

Her aunt clapped briskly. "Well, we can work on all these areas, then. But it's mental magic we should focus on for now, as your skills in force magic have proven adequate thus far."

She tilted her head to the side in confusion. "Come again?"

Emalia grinned. "I'm not surprised that you don't recognize the description. It's part of the Atlantean heritage but one abandoned long ago as our society shifted to trials of combat for advancement. The subtle skills are not well suited for such engagements."

"You sound like Yoda, only with your words in the correct order."

She laughed. "An apt characterization, since we'll work on mind tricks."

Cali frowned. "I won't have to lift rocks with my mind, will I?"

Her mentor cackled in amusement. "Good is telekinesis, yes. But for such things, the time is not right."

She put her forehead down on the table and muttered, "Help me, Obi-Wan Kenobi. Everyone around me has gone insane. You're my only hope."

"So. Is that the path you wish to travel today?"

Cali lifted her head with a sigh. "Tell me more about it."

Emalia shrugged. "It's very much like illusion, but you will manifest the effects in the target's mind, rather than the real world."

She frowned. "So, mind control?"

A stern look grew on her teacher's face. "Only in the most extreme uses, and I would never countenance it except in cases of life and death. More often, it is used to distract, deceive, or occlude."

Her frown expanded. "That still sounds like dark side stuff, Ms Yoda."

Emalia shrugged. "If it allows you to end a situation without fighting, is it not worthwhile?"

A flippant reply jumped to her lips, but she forced herself to really consider the question. The woman's words usually carried depths of meaning. "I'm not sure. I guess as long as I'm not forcing whoever it is to do something they wouldn't do anyway. Like, it wouldn't be okay to make one person kill another."

Her mentor waved her hand. "That isn't possible without years of training, and then only against the weakest-willed people. No, this is more about making them look away at a pivotal moment or perhaps hear something that isn't there. It could even be to take actions, but not ones that would cause them extreme distress."

Thinking back to the recent past, being able to make the Zatora thugs outside the nightclub think they'd missed them would have been extremely useful. Or to have the one guarding the back look the wrong way at the right time. "Is this more dependable than illusion?"

Emalia nodded. "There's always the chance that an illusion will fail at the wrong moment or that it will be detected because it's such a large and powerful spell. These magics are subtle and focused. As such, they are less likely to be noticed."

Cali leaned back and folded her arms. "Great Aunt, you have an evil and manipulative streak in you that I didn't expect but definitely appreciate."

The woman across the table laughed. "You know much less about me than you might think, Caliste. So, is it your desire to learn the way of mental magic?"

The idea of messing with other people's minds made her stomach squirm. *It's one thing to cast an illusion—that's messing with the world, not with individual brains. This is a violation. I'm not sure what kind, but still.* She was about to say no when she remembered the session with Ikehara. If she didn't fully commit, he'd more or less said, she'd lose.

81

And she couldn't afford that, not with the number of people depending on her.

Cali took a deep breath and released it slowly. "Yes. I need to. So, where do we begin?"

Emalia smiled and looked pleased with the answer. "Where we always begin. Clear your mind."

She went through the steps of locking down her whirling thoughts, pushing them into alcoves like the ones at the back of the Dragons, and sealing them in with police caution tape. The process was quicker each time she did it —which was far more often since she'd pushed herself onto the Atlanteans' radar—and in a matter of seconds, she was ready.

Her teacher's voice changed during lessons and became sterner and less understanding. It was a window into how she might have been as a younger woman before the confidence that came with age mellowed her. "Where before, you focused on changing the things around your subject, now you have to change them. I want you to concentrate on me. This is kind of like what we did earlier, where you sent a feeling or idea, but it's different as well. Mental messages are a low-level version of this skill."

She interrupted, "So I'll be able to do telepathy after this?"

Emalia sighed. "Focus, please. Yes, with training, but that's not the point of this session." Cali apologized and put that exciting concept into an alcove with the others. "So. You want me to be distracted by something. If it only manifested in the real world, it might be noticed by those you don't intend to affect, so you have to place it in my mind. More, though, you have to make me susceptible to it.

I could simply ignore it. So, it's two parts simultaneously. First, you change me so I'll be primed to notice it and second, you give me the thing to notice."

Cali closed her eyes and opened her senses. She could hear the other woman's breaths and the way she adjusted her chair and could smell her perfume, along with a general sense of her presence. The scent drew her, and she sent her mind along the path to its source. As she did so, an image of her teacher built in her inner vision and gained resolution and detail as she moved forward. It was like nothing she'd ever experienced, and while she wanted to stay and investigate, the line she followed was too tenuous and fragile to permit any distraction.

She focused harder, now seeking a way into the figure before her. It changed and solid lines became a series of dots as she grew closer, giving her the key. It wasn't about creating a specific entry point but about making her magic small enough to crawl into the spaces that already existed. She concentrated on planting the idea of the shop being open into her mind, then created the sound of the bell that rang when the front door was used.

When Emalia's head twitched in that direction and broke into a smile, she felt it. It was less than she'd wanted but it was something, and for a first step, she'd take it. Her eyes opened to find a grin on her teacher's face.

"Good work, Cali. Remember what you did because the experience is different for everyone. Your magic acts as an interpreter, translating the real world in a way that you can best interact with it. It's unique to you."

She laughed. "Yet one more thing that's unique about me. I'm special, really." The older woman chuckled in response, and Fyre snorted. She frowned at him. "Shut it, you. I don't see you doing mental magic." He opened an eye, winked it slowly, and closed it again.

Emalia said, "I've done some research at the library into Draksa. It's actually quite unique that he can speak out loud. Normally, communication with them is through emotional resonance or, with the most intelligent ones, through a form of telepathy. It's strange that he doesn't use mental magic, actually." Her voice turned playful. "If I had to guess, he thinks you're not sophisticated enough to understand him if he tries to talk mind to mind."

Cali huffed dramatically and stood. "I will not sit here and be insulted."

Her teacher interrupted with a laugh. "Is that why you're standing?"

She growled in mock annoyance. "I will neither sit nor stand here and be insulted. Let's go, Fyre. There are people out there in the square who will actually be nice to us." She extended her tongue at the older woman and drew more laughter. The Draksa climbed to his feet with a catlike stretch and ambled toward the door.

Emalia said, "Be safe, child, and continue to practice what you learned today. Come back as soon as you can, and we'll work on more."

Dropping the act, Cali replied, "You too. Keep an eye out for anything weird. Call me if you need anything—any time."

Her aunt waved at her. "I'm more than capable of handling my own affairs. Off with you."

She looked at Fyre. "Yeah, I wouldn't want to be the

person who thought she was merely an old lady who could be taken advantage of. Crispy-fried-bad-guy."

The Draksa snorted, clearly amused. She opened the door to the sunny afternoon and strode out, already excited to see Dasante and what they could put together to entertain the tourists—some of whom would have the added experience of a little mind magic practice to go with their show.

CHAPTER ELEVEN

She made it through most of the evening shift without incident until the opening door revealed Tanyith. He wasn't in nightclub wear today, only jeans and a t-shirt, which she thought of as his "real" clothes. *I guess I don't really know what's real for him since I've only known him for a couple of weeks.* He took a seat at the bar and began to chat to Zeb. The hunch in his back and the way he held his shoulders conveyed worry.

Cali made sure the customers near her were properly taken care of before she snaked through the loud crowd to join her friends. Tanyith had chosen a soda instead of one of the small glasses, which reinforced the idea that he was concerned about something. She slid into the seat next to him.

Zeb said, "We were waiting for you. He has some questions, and I thought you might be able to weigh in."

The man turned to face her. "Do you know anything about the Stallion Bar?"

She shrugged. "It's fairly low-key and doesn't have the

highest quality clientele. Definitely not a place for the tourists."

The dwarf nodded. "I would describe it the same way. The magical council keeps an eye on it because it's long been a place where humans who are...shall we say, less than accepting of others have gathered."

Tanyith barked a laugh. "That's a gentle way of saying human gang members, right?"

Zeb shrugged. "Another fitting description, sure."

"Do you know whether the Zatoras have taken it over completely? And if so, when?"

Cali frowned. "Why are you so hot on the Stallion?"

He sighed. "It's a long and involved story, but the short version is that I'm being paid to look into someone's disappearance. A magical, in fact, and that person was last seen hanging around that bar. It was a while ago, though. Shortly after I went inside."

The proprietor shook his head. "That's more than enough time for the trail to go cold."

Tanyith nodded. "I'm aware of that. But it's the only lead I have at the moment."

She patted him on the shoulder. "Well, if you need an assist, I'm certainly willing to help you." She paused to let the seemingly kind gesture sink in. "For a percentage. Sixty sounds right."

The two laughed, and they all turned as the front door to the bar banged open. Two men entered, both of whom she recognized from the night they'd brought the gangs together at the Dragons. They were the ones who had accompanied the leader of the Zatora syndicate. One was thin and intelligent-looking but still carried an aura of danger. The other was clearly muscle. Both appeared to have weapons hidden under their jackets.

They surveyed the room with sharp eyes before one moved forward to stand near the bar and the other stepped aside from where he blocked the entrance. Their boss, Rion Grisham, stepped into the tavern with a sour expression. He wore a brown suit that looked more expensive than any ten things she'd ever owned over tan and brown shoes that probably cost as much as the rest of her wardrobe put together. His face was clean-shaven, and it would be easy to mistake him for a corporate executive if you caught him without his muscle at hand.

He walked forward and leaned on the side of the bar, putting him between Zeb and Tanyith from her angle. Her muscles tensed, and she realized belatedly that there was something about him that scared her. Maybe it was the way he'd yanked them off the street on a whim. *Or maybe it's that he has every reason to want revenge on us for breaking into his place. And he seems like someone who doesn't make a habit of letting things go easily.*

Zeb was smooth, as always. "Greetings, Mr Grisham. What will you and your friends have?"

The man responded with a thin smile. "Only words for now, Zarden." He looked at each of them in turn. "Mr Shale. Ms Leblanc." Their names came out like a threat—or a promise.

The dwarf asked, "Are you here to use the Dragons as neutral territory, then? No other factions are present at the moment."

He shook his head and leaned in a little further as if to

share information he didn't want others to hear. "No, it's you three I wish to speak to—and of."

Damn. That's not good. She met Zeb's eyes, and he inclined his head slightly to the left, which she took as a negative reply. *Okay. We'll let it play out.* She reached inside and touched her magic but didn't bring it forward. The man between the door and the bar stepped six inches closer as if he, too, wanted to hear what Grisham would say.

The Zatora leader tapped his index finger on the wooden surface as he spoke. "That little trick with the disguises was quite clever. It threw us off the scent for a day but you couldn't actually have thought we'd believe the stolen items somehow randomly wound up here. Come on, give us credit for some intelligence, anyway."

Zeb shrugged and Tanyith remained silent. She did the same, although the snarky comment about his brainpower that had raced from her head to her tongue challenged her restraint.

"So, two disguised individuals came into my house and messed with my things, which wound up at this bar. It just so happens I had two people from this bar in my house not a week before. That kind of coincidence is difficult to ignore."

Tanyith shrugged. "Still, the universe is a random place."

Grisham showed his teeth in a grim smile. "I've built a career on believing everything is connected. Sure, there's been a mistake or two along the way, but most of the time, it proves true. So I'm here to put you on notice." He turned his head to face Zeb. "I haven't decided what my response to the invasion will be. Maybe I'll take a piece of the earnings from this place under the table so no one will think your precious neutrality is violated. You'll hear my decision before too long."

Her flinch at the man's words caused Tanyith to touch her knee. The speaker didn't seem to notice or didn't care if he did. He simply returned his gaze to the two of them. "You two, on the other hand, had better stay out of my way. If I or one of my people sees you anywhere you shouldn't be, you can count on it turning into trouble." He raised a palm to stop her as she opened her mouth to speak. "Shh. Don't say a word. You might live longer."

He straightened, nodded to Zeb, and exited the bar. His lieutenants backed out behind him. They were silent until he had departed, then Tanyith sighed loudly. "Gee, that went well."

Zeb shrugged. "It was inevitable. But it's not worth worrying about, other than to take him at his word and plan accordingly."

"So you think we should let him go?" she demanded. "Let him get away with threatening us like that?"

Tanyith stood. "No chance. Is there a back door out of here?"

After Cali had escorted him out, Tanyith used a burst of force magic to carry him to the top of the building two stories above. He recognized the same limo that had picked them up halfway down the street, headed in a different direction than the mansion. *Excellent. Let's see what you're up to, Grisham.*

He repeated the magic to launch himself from roof to roof, choosing vectors that would keep him out of sight of pedestrians and traffic below. When he had to cross a big intersection, he shrouded himself in illusion before he did so and hopefully ensured that he would seem like a ripple in the night sky if anyone noticed his passing. His skills in illusion and veils were not particularly impressive as he'd always been a charge in and meet the challenge head-on kind of person.

As he followed the car, his mind wandered and he considered the three women who populated his life at the moment. Sienna appeared to be the same as ever, and despite the hope that had prodded him to ask her out, he had changed enough that reconnecting romantically might be difficult. Cali had the potential to grow into a good friend, especially if they continued to do stupid things together. Her drive was completely unlike See's go with the flow attitude. The fact that the young woman studied an indirect martial art seemed at odds with what he knew about her.

Finally, Barton was like a grown-up, jaded version of Cali—aggressive, no-nonsense, but smart and wielding a wicked tongue. Most of the time, he found her as abrasive as hell, but he had to admit her head was mostly in the right place. Except where his status as a former gang member was concerned.

He crouched on a rooftop when the car stopped at an unremarkable building among a cluster of old warehouses. It was three stories or so high with a peaked roof. The first level was all cement block and the second and third were constructed using metal sheets. The structure was entirely industrial and made a strange juxtaposition with the limo that stood outside waiting for an oversized garage door to roll out of the way. When it did, the vehicle pulled in out of sight and the rolling barrier closed ponderously behind it.

Tanyith could have made it inside with a leap and a dash and some magic, but he didn't possess that level of impulsiveness. He resigned himself to a long wait for them to emerge. It made zero sense to investigate the location while they were present. He had finally found a comfortable place to sit when a thump sounded from across the rooftop. His adrenaline surged as he scrambled to his feet to discover the Draksa looking at him with its tongue hanging out.

Before he could say anything, soft cursing emanated from the side of the building and he peered over the edge to find Cali scaling the fire escape. When she reached the top, she pointed at Fyre. "You need to carry a climbing rope or something. Or maybe a saddle so I can ride on your back. I'm tired of running around dodging people and cars and trying to follow your scaly ass while you soar overhead."

He snorted and she scowled at the creature again. She turned to face him and laughed at his expression. "What? You didn't think I would let you handle this on your own, did you?"

CHAPTER TWELVE

C ali hated every second of waiting for the Zatoras to leave the building but knew Tanyith was right—it was the smart play. That didn't diminish the way it chafed against her nerves, though. *The bastard comes into our place and threatens us? He needs to be taken down a peg or three.*

She held rationality at arm's length and let her emotions burn, hoping they'd consume themselves and allow her to think more clearly. Aiming for a balance of cold logic and hot instinct had always worked for her but right now, she had more of the latter than she needed. *Scumbag.* She shook her head and sighed.

The Draksa leaned against her where he sat on her left and pushed her into Tanyith. He pushed back, and she transmitted the motion to Fyre. They'd played this stupid game for almost fifteen minutes, and she was ready to kill them both. The slap she was about to deliver to both heads was preempted by the sounds of the garage door opening below.

Together, they snuck forward to peer over the edge.

Sure enough, the limo was pulling away. She gave the building one more cursory scan to match the seven or eight she'd already done. It had no windows and only the garage door and one other entry point on the ground level. The peaked roof provided no clear access inside. Presumably, there'd be more on the far side but since that faced the river, they'd be more visible in their approach. Tanyith had agreed that to use the main door or the garage was the better way to go.

She led the others down the fire escape on the opposite side of the building, and they walked through the alley. Cali pictured two of the other Atlanteans she'd seen pictures of and created a hasty disguise over her and Tanyith, trusting Fyre to take care of his own visibility. They crossed the street at a slow amble, merely a couple of ordinary folks out for a walk in the deserted warehouse district. He raised a hand and the camera that slowly panned above the door froze in place, pointed away from them.

When she tried the handle, it was locked, although that wasn't a surprise. Tanyith removed the same device he'd used before from his pocket and jammed it against the lock. Moments later, he turned the knob to let them in. She paused so Fyre could sneak through the opening, then closed it quietly behind them. What had appeared to be three floors from the outside was clearly less on the inside, as the one they were on extended vertically for at least a story and a half. Palettes of boxed goods wrapped in heavy plastic were arranged in rows and columns in the back half of the space. The section to their left was where the limo had pulled in, and there was an open area on their right that included a metal staircase leading up through the ceiling.

She whispered, "This place is way too big and way too filled up for comfort. Stolen stuff, maybe?"

Tanyith nodded. "Most likely. Apparently, the gang has all kinds of diverse things going on—more than we thought."

Fyre had already moved to the staircase, so she followed him up as quietly as she was able and rolled her feet carefully from heel to toe with each step. At the top was an entirely different arrangement. Where the downstairs was wide open, the stairs ended in a room with a heavy door blocking the path to the larger portion of the building. Beside that door, a man with a rifle surged to his feet at her appearance. Fyre had moved out of the line of fire, and she punched the air to deliver a fist of force to his midsection. He doubled over with a loud "oomph" but started to raise the weapon as he straightened. By then, she was beside him and pushed on his arms to lift the gun higher. His shots went into the ceiling when he pressed the trigger.

She held onto his wrist, spun under his arms, and thrust her right elbow into his ribs. As a follow-up, she stamped on the top of his foot, and when he shifted his balance reflexively, she yanked his arms down and over her to flip him. His rifle clattered away as he landed hard. Tanyith knelt beside the fallen thug and withdrew zip ties from his pocket to bind the guard's hands and feet together.

Cali crouched beside him. "You actually carry zip ties around?"

He shrugged. "After what we've been through lately?

Yeah. You never know. Plus, if you're arrested with them, they're far more explainable than handcuffs."

She shook her head. "Do you think anyone heard the shots?"

Tanyith nodded. "For sure. I can't imagine they'd have only one person on guard. If they cared enough to guard it, they would have cared enough to have multiple people."

"Plan?"

"I don't think either of us has enough mojo to blast that door off its hinges. It's probably on a heavy steel frame bolted to the floor and to a crossbeam. So I'll have to pick the lock. Then you can pull it open, and I'll charge in."

"How good are your shields?"

He sighed and shook his head. "Adequate. Plus, this was my idea, so I'll go first. No complaining."

She laughed. "Gotcha, boss. You do whatever your maleness requires you to do, no matter how stupid."

Grumbling under his breath, he pulled the device out and inserted it into the lock again. It hummed slightly before the latch clicked and he repeated the process with the deadbolt above. She whispered, "What is that?"

Tanyith grinned. "It's a power lock pick gun. I stole it from a government locksmith a long time ago. It works like a charm on most simple ones."

"What do you do for complex locks?"

"Blast them away with magic. Pull the door on three." He counted on his fingers, and she yanked the barrier aside as the last one came down. When he surged into the room, the rifle reports indicated four shots in rapid succession. She followed him in, raised a force shield in front of her, and discovered a long hallway with doorways set into either side. Her partner was three-quarters of the way down it, and the man who had shot at him was falling, apparently the victim of a magical attack.

She had a moment of relief at the ease of the victory before two men appeared in the middle of the corridor, one from each side. The first turned toward Tanyith, and she attacked him with a growl and threw a force punch at him. The other closed quickly and by the time his partner went down, his fist had already covered most of the distance to her face.

There was no time to block so she yanked her head in the same direction in which the blow traveled. With both motions in sync, the impact was far less damaging when it landed than it would have been. Still, it careened her toward the wall and a painful collision with another heavy metal door powerful enough to make it chime. Fyre growled but she knew the man was too close for her ally to act. A quick push off the cold surface to deliver a side-kick solved that problem, and as soon as he staggered away from her, the Draksa locked him in magical ice.

She dropped to one knee and took stock of herself. *Brain still working? Check. Body still working? Check. Sense of superiority smashed? Check.* It had been a while since she'd taken a blow to the face, and it was always a shock when it happened. She shook her head, pleased to find that it didn't hurt, and pushed herself to her feet. On the way, her gaze swept across an open slot in the door, and she recoiled at the sight of a pair of eyes looking at her. "Holy hell, what the actual—" She stopped herself from finishing the sentence.

Tanyith was at her side in an instant. "What?"

"There's someone in there." She pointed at the door. He frowned, leaned forward and looked inside, and nodded. He retrieved the tool to unlock it and dragged the heavy barrier open slowly. Shrouded in the shadows was a man—a teenager or perhaps a little older—in ragged shorts and nothing else. His hair was in tight, dirty braids, and the room stank like he'd been there for a while. He shrank back against the wall.

"It's okay," Tanyith said, "we're here to help. Can you tell me your name?"

He shook his head slightly. Cali whispered, "He looks like he's in shock. Do you think he's an Atlantean?"

Her partner held his hands up to show he wasn't hiding anything and backed from the room, leaving the door open behind him. The enraged look on his face provided the answer before he said it. "Definitely." He gestured to a long line of similar doors. "I bet these are some of the people who came in on the cruise ships. Maybe not everyone is greeted by the gang or something."

"You don't think these are captive gang members?"

He shook his head. "He has no ink and if they are all like him, they don't seem resilient enough to have worked on the streets. They're probably new arrivals that the damn Zatoras snatched before they could make contact—or who some bastard on the docks sold out to them."

She winced. "You don't think there could be someone in New Atlantis working with them, do you? Like, human trafficking? Er…Atlantean trafficking?"

"No." There was no doubt in his tone. "They wouldn't work with humans on such a thing. No Atlantean would. If this was a warehouse owned by the local Atlanteans, I might believe it was possible. But this? No chance."

Fyre snorted, and it made her realize she'd lost track of things. "We need to get the rest of these cells open." They took the doors in sequence. He unlocked them and moved on to the next while she opened them and talked to whoever was inside. By the end, they had found an even dozen prisoners, two-thirds male, most of whom were unwilling to leave their chambers. Two were, however, and Tanyith drew them to the corner and handed them the rifles they'd confiscated. Immediately, the duo seemed more assured, perhaps discarding the notion that it was all an elaborate trap. *He's smarter than he looks. Where people other than women are concerned, anyway.*

"Where did you come from?" Tanyith asked.

The first—a man who looked to be about his age and had a dirty beard and bald head—replied in an accent that sounded like the Caribbean. "New Atlantis by way of Jamaica."

She tilted her head. "Why?"

He looked at her, his height giving him what she considered an unfair advantage in the discussion. "Culture shock is easier to deal with that way. We live above the waters for a while, then come here where it's so different."

She and her partner nodded in unison. He said, "That makes sense. It explains some things, actually, since I wondered how the New Atlanteans would get aboard the cruise ships."

The former prisoner stood comfortably with the rifle in his hands like he knew how to use it. While at first, she had imagined the prisoners to be weak, she now realized it was merely having been held captive that made them seem so. His muscles were ropy and powerful-looking, and he had an attitude that showed little fear.

"How long have you been here?" she asked,

He shrugged. "They used drugs to put us to sleep and to wake us up, so I have no way to know. It doesn't matter, though. What's important is that you have freed us. Can you take us to Usha?"

Tanyith barked a short laugh. "Not so much. What we can do is leave the doors open so you can make your own way and tell you how to get there. The truth is that she doesn't like us very much at the moment." The man looked interested, and he simply shook his head. "It's a long story. Suffice it to say we're not on good terms."

The other man extended a hand. Tanyith reached forward, and instead of grasping it, grabbed higher up on the man's arm. The Atlantean reciprocated with a nod, then gestured with the rifle down the hallway. "You should go now in case the shots bring people. We can take care of our own from here." The other man, who was smaller, stockier, and had a full head of curly hair, nodded. He said, "Thank you," in a harsh rasp that sounded like it hurt.

"You're welcome," she replied. "Will thirty minutes be enough time for you to escape?"

The man nodded and waved as they departed. Once they were several blocks away, they ducked into an alley and emerged on the far side, no longer disguised. Tanyith asked, "Why the time limit?"

She shrugged. "I worked on that coincidence thing. If the police arrive, maybe it'll cover the fact that it was us who broke Grisham's prisoners out."

He laughed. "Plus, you'll earn cred with Barton."

Cali shook her head and pulled out the prepaid phone she'd had Dasante purchase for her. "Nope. Anonymous tip." She gave him a sly smile. "Although, you know, if you're looking for ways to get her to like you, I don't mind if you call it in."

He rolled his eyes and walked faster. She laughed and turned to Fyre. "It's not only me, right? Those two are at least a little interested in each other."

He nodded with his tongue out and his face amused, and she hurried to catch up, calling, "So, do you want to reach out to her, or should I?"

CHAPTER THIRTEEN

It had crept up on her so suddenly that Cali had completely forgotten and only the notice on the wall the evening before had reminded her. *The Drunken Dragons Tavern will be closed for a private event on Thursday night.*

That private event was her birthday, and it was an important one. The year before had been notable, as she'd moved into her United States legal majority at eighteen and could do things like vote and work in bars. But this year—nineteen—was the one her birth culture, the Atlanteans, considered to be the most important one, the true transition into adulthood.

Emalia and Zeb had insisted on a celebration, and who was she to argue? The guest list had grown by the day— friends of her late parents, friends of her great aunt, notable customers, some of her classmates, and several of her busking comrades. And Tanyith, of course. She'd offered to let him bring a plus one and suggested he could invite Barton, but he'd demurred with an eye-roll so powerful they'd almost fallen out of his head.

She and Fyre walked from the boardinghouse to the bar among the early evening revelers. No one took particular notice of the redhead in jeans and a t-shirt and the white Rottweiler that marched beside her. The Draksa had taken to changing his color scheme every time they ventured out and frankly, she couldn't blame him. If she was capable of transforming her looks so easily, she'd do it too.

Of course, she could simply use illusion, but that required concentration and focus and she didn't wish to expend her reserves of either on frivolous things. *Well, not on such normal frivolous things. A good prank, though, would be worth it.* She had considered that putting a pair of magical invisible bunny ears on Zeb for the party might be a good idea but she'd decided that Tanyith would make a much better target—unless he came with someone she didn't want to embarrass him in front of.

Then, she'd reconsidered once again because not everyone at the party knew she was magical and it was probably safer for them to remain unaware. Although she expected that at a minimum, Zeb's Dark Elf friend would be present, it was likely to be a mostly human gathering, so it probably made sense to keep the arcane stuff on the down-low.

Nineteen. Wow. I wish you could be here to see it. Her parents were never far from her thoughts but even during her childhood, this particular event had loomed large for her as it did for all Atlantean children. In that society, one's life path began at the age of maturity, and most didn't deviate much from their initial trajectory. She had thought about being a healer, at first, and later, a politician. Now, she imagined she would probably have chosen something akin to investigation had she been able to grow up inside that culture. Puzzles had always appealed to her.

She gazed at her companion, who strode happily down the street. Fyre was almost entirely metallic, and his scales were gorgeous in the setting sun. She didn't have any real memories of New Atlantis but occasionally imagined what it might be like to walk around and see more Draksa or other amazing creatures along the way. Certainly, she liked New Orleans, but she definitely wasn't against the idea of a vacation trip to the homeland.

Well, maybe now that I'm nineteen I can put that together. She snorted internally. Unless she came into a windfall or made some unlikely friends, she wouldn't visit New Atlantis anytime soon. Portals to the undersea city weren't exactly widely available, and she wasn't in the right economic class at the moment to book a cruise that would take her there.

The area outside the tavern was uncharacteristically empty, with only a few people wandering about. She looked surreptitiously at the areas where the Atlantean gang members had lurked but didn't see any. A metal post with a jagged edge protruded from a telephone pole, which suggested they'd taken down another of the Zatoras' cameras or maybe a police camera. There was no way to tell who was watching these days, so she simply assumed that everyone was.

She pulled the door open and headed into the tavern, inspiring a loud cheer with her appearance. Cali grinned at the crowd of well-wishers and released Fyre's leash so he could scamper to his usual space behind the bar. She crossed to Zeb, who stood on his chair and leaned over the wooden counter to give her a hug. "Happy birthday, girl."

"Thank you. And thanks for this."

He shrugged and took his seat, but a smile tugged at the corners of his mouth. "It's no big deal. I'll simply take the lost profits out of your paycheck. You'll never notice."

She made a goofy face at him and descended the three wide stairs into the main part of the room. Dasante was the first to greet her, dressed in a tuxedo t-shirt with his arms bare, and the jeans he'd claimed were the nicest he owned. She laughed and took his hand to move through their personal handshake that ended with a chest bump. "D. Thanks for coming."

He held one of the evening's snacks up, a grilled cheese sandwich. Panini presses ran down an entire long table, with rented chefs ready to make custom sandwiches. "I wouldn't have missed a free meal, you know that."

"Whatever the excuse, I'm glad you're here. Did you bring friends?" He nodded and pointed out a few people she hadn't met. "Excellent. Introduce me." Making contacts among the other street performers was always a good thing and doubly so if she could get a little credit for their invitation to the party. It would make working together later easier.

As she chatted with them, Zeb called her name. She turned to find Detective Kendra Barton standing beside him and suppressed a reflexive scowl before she walked up the steps again and extended a hand to the detective. When she took it, Cali tasted mainly pineapple tinged with banana, which suggested that while Barton wished her well overall, she still had suspicions. *Fine, that makes us even, more or less.* "How are you tonight, Detective?"

She shrugged. "Good, Cali. It's polite of you to ask." The woman grinned as if she knew how irritating she was. "I only wanted to stop by and wish you a happy nineteenth." She leaned in and spoke in a tone that wouldn't carry. "And also to say thanks for the tip. Don't bother denying it. There are no other citizens at the moment who are willing to stand up to the gangs. Maybe eventually, there will be more." She didn't confirm or deny the statement and the detective plowed on. "Anyway, we found four Atlanteans there and they're now in the hospital being taken care of. I assume there were more."

She automatically moved to argue and Barton shook her head. "It doesn't matter, either way. If there were, they hopefully made it somewhere safe where they won't cause trouble." Cali kept her face neutral. *Not exactly.*

When the detective didn't continue speaking, she replied, "I'm sure I don't know what you're talking about. But if I did, I'd say you're welcome." She smiled, and the other woman returned it. "Will you stay for the party? I think Tanyith will be here later." She put a verbal leer into the last sentence, and the woman mimed gagging herself with a finger, which made them both laugh. "Well, you're allowed to stay anyway."

She shook her head. "No thanks. Work calls. This happened to be on my route today." The brunette took a moment to say goodbye to Zeb and headed out the door.

Cali turned to the dwarf. "That was a little weird, don't you think?"

He shrugged. "Weird is basically normal around here

these days. I wouldn't say she's any stranger than the group of people you've brought together here. Speaking of which, go save Emalia from Invel before he talks her ears off."

She swung around with a laugh to search for the Dark Elf. She found him facing a corner, her great aunt trapped between him and the wall. Cali caught her eye and walked at a snail's pace toward them, earning an exasperated glare. Finally, she arrived and tapped the Drow on the shoulder. He turned, and she noticed the mottled skin that Zeb had mentioned once in describing him. She thought the imperfection improved his looks, rather than detracted from them.

"Oh, hello, birthday woman. Congratulations on your majority."

Cali nodded. "Thank you and thank you so much for coming. Zeb asked me to have you come talk to him. Between you and me, I think he's a little lonely there by himself. Fyre's not a particularly engaging conversationalist."

Invel perked up and replied, "Certainly." He turned and gave a short bow to Emalia, who nodded in return, and departed for the front of the room, his stately walk punctuated with a slight limp.

She broke into laughter. "So, were you chatting long?"

The older woman sighed. "He's absolutely charming but we don't travel in the same circles and have little in common. I think he was trying to work up the nerve to ask for a reading but never managed it. He did invite me to view the items in his store sometime."

"You know that he trades in pieces of…uh, questionable origin, right?"

Her great aunt grinned. "Well, certainly. That's how you get the best bargains."

Cali blinked in surprise, then scowled as the woman laughed at her. "Stop messing my birthday up. You're supposed to be nice to me today, for a change."

It only made her mentor laugh harder. "Ah, child, I am entirely too nice to you on all days. That's why you've turned out to be such a troublemaker."

The door opened, and she threw a quick look over her shoulder. "Speaking of troublemaker, hang on. Tay," she called, "get over here."

He saw her and obeyed, and she introduced him. "Emalia, Tanyith. Tanyith, Emalia. She's my great aunt. He's my sometimes partner in troublemaking."

She nodded and extended a hand, which he shook dutifully. "So he's replaced Dasante?"

Cali laughed. "This is an entirely different kind of troublemaking."

"I thought so. You're the one who's not so strong at disguises, then?"

Tanyith chuckled as she groaned and put her face in her hands. "Yes, that's me, although I'm not sure I'd describe it quite that way."

Cali's muffled voice said, "Thanks, Emalia. Really."

The older woman chuckled. "Be off with you. I need to talk to Caliste for a second."

She groaned again at the use of her full name and pulled her face out of her hands as he wandered off. "What?"

She smiled. "You know your parents would be very proud of you today, right?" Emotion surged, so she merely nodded rather than trying to speak. "In their place, a certain duty has fallen to me. You must visit me tomorrow at noon, at which time I will give you the remaining things they left for you."

"There's more?" She frowned. "Why didn't you include them when you gave me the necklace and rings?"

The woman raised a finger. "Not the same kinds of things. Your magic is fully unfettered so I'm not referring to that. Rather, it's their legacy for you."

"Something to remember them by, I guess."

Emalia's face turned serious. "Oh, no, Caliste. Hardly that. This is your inheritance we're talking about. Now, go and enjoy your party. But don't be late."

She tried to pry more information from her, but the woman wouldn't budge. The rest of the night was wonderful but all of it was colored by the mystery lurking in the back of her mind. *What did they leave behind for me and more importantly, what does it mean for my future?*

CHAPTER FOURTEEN

Only the diversion of the dojo kept Cali from endless wondering about what her parents might have left for her. The night's sleep had been brittle and frequently broken as her brain spewed a new theory. In the end, she'd given up halfway through the night and done homework instead.

Ikehara must have sensed her distraction because he pushed her harder than usual, which allowed her to lose herself in the fight. Even the group session was intense enough that others commented on it. She realized that once again, he'd found a way to help her without questioning why she needed assistance. Her sensei was a treasure.

Fyre had waited outside during the public class, and they walked unhurriedly together toward Emalia's shop. With forty-five minutes in which to cover twenty minutes' worth of ground, she had a good opportunity for people-watching. She'd exhausted the interesting stores on the route months before. There weren't many and she didn't have enough cash for frivolous purchases anyway. Hearing the stories of some of the characters who showed up to busk in hopes of buying this or that fancy item, she thought she was probably lucky not to have to worry about that stuff. As long as she had her phone, a working computer, and someone else's Wi-Fi to share, she was set. *Well, and an occasional replacement t-shirt for when an ambushing idiot slashes mine with a knife.* Today's faded selection, advertising The Who, had come from a thrift store.

Fyre had seemed more himself since his solo outing. She'd given him hell for leaving without letting her know but it had been mainly bluster and worry for his safety. He was still bothered, she thought, but had at least made a temporary peace with his lack of knowledge.

Her thoughts caused the trip to pass quickly, and she arrived with fifteen minutes to spare. Fortunately, Dasante was on the corner, setting up his magic table. He was one of the hardest working performers on the square, arriving early and staying late most days. If not for the job at the tavern and her classes, she would doubtless compete with him to see who was more dedicated. He had a comedy routine that he pulled out later in the evening when there were fewer children around to hear the hilarious but curse-filled jokes and stories.

As always, he turned as she neared. She wasn't sure how he knew when she was coming, but he seemed to. *Maybe it's like a busker Spidey Sense. It warns of friends or enemies.* His smile pulled a matching expression from her. "Hey, D."

"Hey yourself." They performed their greeting routine and he took a step back and made a point of studying her outfit. "New shirt?"

She nodded. "I found a Ziggy Stardust one, too. Someone must have cleaned out their closet."

"Nice." He jerked his head in the direction of his table and turned back to his preparations. She circled so she'd be in his line of sight. "It looks like it'll be a good day—cool but sunny. There should be a ton of folks around. Are you gonna stay and work?"

Cali shook her head. She hadn't told anyone about Emalia's revelation but felt compelled to share with him. "My great aunt has something for me from my parents. I'm supposed to show up at high noon."

He made a whistle like in a western, and they both laughed. When times were slow, they watched dumb videos on YouTube and had found one with whistles from over a hundred films and television shows compiled into a single reel. They'd giggled like idiots for a quarter of an hour over how repetitive it was. "That's heavy stuff. Are you okay?"

Dasante had a way of offering support that never seemed to consider her weaker for taking it. She nodded. "Yeah, for now. I might be a train wreck later, depending on what the big mystery turns out to be."

"I can see that." D had grown up without a father, and when his mother had remarried a man with younger kids, had chosen to spend most of his time away from them. There was no particular animosity in him, only a "lack of interest for the whole scene." She couldn't relate as she would have given up everything she owned for only one more day with her own parents, but she didn't press him on it. He was a great friend to her and she did her best to be the same for him.

Her phone chimed with a five-minute warning, and she nodded and walked toward the shop. It wasn't goodbye since they both knew she'd go directly to him after to share the news, good or bad. He gave Fyre a pat on the head as he passed, and the illusory Rottweiler barked in return.

When she entered the shop, Emalia was waiting. She was garbed in a long dress that puddled on the floor at her feet, appropriate for a wedding or a funeral. The darkened room of her customer area was steeped in solemnity today. Cali's eyes snapped to the large box in front of her great aunt. It was made of a kind of wood she didn't recognize that seemed to glow with an inner light. Different shades rippled through it like someone had dropped a stone into a pond.

The older woman gestured for her to take the chair across from her, and she complied. Fyre ducked under the purple cloth that covered the table and banged against her feet as he arranged himself. She shared a small grin with Emalia at his behavior before the weight of the moment descended on her and she straightened her spine and took a deep breath.

"So, Caliste. You have reached your majority. In Atlantean society, this is the time when one chooses their own path forward. You were forced to make that decision a little early, I think, but I would say you are moving in the best direction for you."

She nodded, fully aware she hadn't said "the right direction." Emalia had always refused to judge her choices in that way, only helped her along whatever route she chose on her own. "I hope so."

The other woman smiled. "Most of the time, that's all

we can do. The future is shrouded in fog and mist. The past, though"—she ran a hand across the top of the box —"on occasion, has the ability to inform us of what is to come. Hopefully, that will be the case for you today."

Confused, she tilted her head to the side. "You don't know what's in there?"

Her mentor shook her head slowly. "I do not. This is usually a moment shared only by parents and child. I am honored and saddened to be a part of yours."

Cali wiped the tears from her eyes before they could trickle out on their own. "I'm sad that I can't have them but glad that I have you."

Emalia nodded. "Are you ready?"

She blew out a breath. "As ready as I'll ever be."

"Put your hands on the top of the box."

She leaned forward and obeyed. The surface grew warmer under her palms, and the sensation of movement on the lid was entirely freaky as if the solid material had suddenly become something entirely different. When it cooled again, she pulled her hands away to discover that what had seemed a seamless slab of wood on the top had begun to fold back upon itself. In moments, the box was open, but all she could see inside was a piece of dark fabric.

Emalia spoke quietly. "Normally, the parents would retrieve the items and explain them. Would you like me to do that for you, or would you like to look on your own? I can leave the room if you'd prefer."

"No." The urgent word pushed past her lips before her mind caught up. "No, I definitely want you to stay. Please, do what they would have done." Again, she dashed tears away, but they were bigger than before and she knew she had almost no chance of making it through the revelations without weeping. As if he sensed her emotions, Fyre put his head on her feet and his presence lent her comfort.

As her aunt reached into the box, Cali noticed unfamiliar jewelry on her fingers—ornate rings she hadn't seen before. The stones were equally unidentifiable, but the settings were similar enough that they were clearly pieces of a set. The first item that emerged from the box was a piece of black fabric. She leaned forward to examine it, and Emalia chuckled warmly. "It's merely a cover. Don't be nervous, Caliste."

She echoed the laughter. "How can I not be nervous?"

The other woman gave her a smile tinged with understanding and sympathy. "True. Okay, here we go." She removed a palm-sized booklet and handed it over. Cali took it and examined the embossed cover. It held the name and logo of Hancock Whitney, one of the oldest banks in New Orleans. The inside displayed a long string of numbers with a small key taped to one page. She folded it open to show it to Emalia, who nodded in recognition. "A safe deposit key. We'll have to discover which branch, to start with."

One more mystery. Nothing's easy. She shook her head. "Okay, what's next?" She set the booklet on the table. A wide fabric ribbon emerged inch by inch as her great aunt pulled it from the box. At the end was another key with something on the round part that caught the light. Cali took it. A number was cut into the metal. "One-six-oh-one?"

Emalia shrugged. "I have no idea about that one. But we'll find the answer eventually, have no worries. Maybe something else in the box will help it to make sense." She withdrew an object wrapped in a scarlet cloth. It stretched from her fingertips to her wrist when she extended it. Cali accepted the bundle, set it on the table, and unwrapped it slowly. Inside was a piece of metal with a smooth, sharp edge on the left. The other sides were jagged and broken. It was covered with etchings that seemed somehow familiar. She rummaged through her recent memories and made the connection. "These markings are like the sword we found in the Atlanteans' club."

The older woman's eyes widened. "That raises more questions than it answers."

She laughed. "Right? I only have about four hundred and seven at the moment, but I'm sure I can come up with more."

Her mentor shook her head. "This is a troubling development. It could be ceremonial and thus only symbolically powerful or an artifact with powers of its own—or anything in between. We definitely need to investigate its origins."

"Yes. After we finish emptying the box."

Emalia laughed. "Of course." The next item to emerge was a small case. Inside was a choker necklace in a fabric that resembled lace but felt like metal in her hands. Silver discs slightly wider in diameter than the black material were set at roughly an inch and a half intervals all the way around. She didn't see a clasp of any kind and pulled on it, surprised that it stretched. She went to slide it over her head and her companion caught her hands.

A frown settled on her face. "Caliste. We don't put potentially magical items around our necks without adequate precautions, even if they came in a box from your parents."

Adrenaline surged through her at the near-miss. Magical history abounded with stories of such traps. *That was an amateur move, Cali. Good going.* She shook her head and set it carefully on the table. "You're right. I'm an idiot."

The other woman looked rattled as well. "It's probably safe, as this came directly from your mother's hands to mine. But still, we should be careful. I will take care of the necessary detection spells when we're finished."

A small pouch was next, made of the same fabric as the necklace. She loosened the drawstrings and reached inside carefully to extract a disc that matched the ones on the choker. It had a colorful design on it, and after staring at it for a moment, she realized it was an Atlantean rune. She'd seen them on Emalia's tarot cards before, always buried deep in the background or otherwise hidden. She held it out to the woman. "What does it mean?"

Her teacher squinted. "Shield." Cali gave her a look and she shrugged. "My first guess is that it's a magical charm like a stored spell. It might need a verbal trigger or a touch, or maybe even simply a thought. We won't know until we—"

She interrupted with a sigh. "Research it. Yeah, I get it."

Emalia grinned. "There are no shortcuts, Caliste."

"But I want some. Pleeease?" she whined.

At a snort from under the table, she stretched a hand down to pet the Draksa. Her aunt peered into the box and said, "Only one item left." She removed a medium-sized book and passed it to her. Cali took it and was immediately struck by the texture of the leather cover. It was smooth and supple and wonderful. She flipped it to the front and saw an embossed symbol—the same compass she wore on her necklace. Again, when she looked at the other woman, all she received was a shrug.

Great, one more mystery. She opened the book and sighed. *Of course.* The interior pages were covered with writing made up of letters and symbols she'd never seen before. She held it open to Emalia. "Atlantean?"

The older woman shook her head. "No. I don't recognize it. But we'll identify it together." She stretched across the table and grabbed one of her hands. "I know this might seem like too much, but we'll discover the meaning of every item. You have my solemn promise and you know I never break my word."

The tears finally escaped. It felt less like sadness and more like closure—or maybe purging of emotions long buried. "I love you."

Emalia nodded and squeezed harder. "And I you."

Fyre rubbed his face against her legs. For a moment, she sensed the presence of her parents and pictured them watching over her from above. *And you. I love and miss you so much. Thank you for these things. I'll remember you always through them.*

CHAPTER FIFTEEN

She and Emalia had tried the nearest bank branch to where she and her parents had lived and discovered that the code and the key gained them access into the vault. Inside the safe deposit box were materials detailing all their financials—including a trust that would provide her with enough money each month that she'd no longer have to worry about whether a given day of busking was good or bad. There was a pile of ledgers she hadn't had time to look at and probably wouldn't anytime soon.

Cali had taken everything, using a large backpack Emalia had brought—pink and dotted with unicorns, unfortunately—and returned in a daze to the shop after she'd arranged a debit card to access the trust. Her great aunt had held onto the bag since she had only an hour or two before she had to be at the tavern to work.

Finally, she stumbled outside with Fyre, who'd waited at her aunt's home while she visited the bank, and found Dasante. He took one look at her and brought his magician patter to a quick close, then guided her over to sit near the fence. Quietly, he lowered himself beside her, his longer legs resting against hers. The Rottweiler Draksa sat on the opposite side of her and looked at the passersby. D snapped his fingers in front of her face. "Hey. Earth to Cal. Are you in there?"

She laughed. "I'm here. It's...so much to take in."

"Tell me." She explained the day's happenings to him. He listened quietly, although he did hold a hand up for a high-five at the revelation of the money her parents had left her. When she had finished, he said, "Okay, so you're basically the same as you were yesterday but with a little extra cash and some stuff to research during your free time, right?"

When she considered it that way, it all seemed much more manageable. "Yeah. I guess you're right."

"But maybe you could be different now, if you wanted to?"

She shrugged. "I don't think that's something I want. I like my life, at least when idiots aren't trying to mess with my people."

Fyre barked in her face and Dasante laughed. "He appears to feel differently."

Cali scowled. "He's a whiner and seems to be of the opinion that my room at the boarding house is too confining. It's not my fault he's so damn big."

Her friend laughed again. "That is a problem. You should have adopted a smaller pet." She'd told him she was concerned about safety and had decided to get a tough dog. He had no idea that the truth was the other way around—that Fyre had essentially adopted her. "There are apartments in my building that aren't too pricey. And I know the owner."

She raised an eyebrow at him. "It sounds sketchy. Are all the other tenants as strange as you?"

"Yep. It's totally your kind of place. You'll fit right in."

She turned to her "pet." "How about it, Fyre? Should we have a look?"

His bark was clearly an affirmative and drew a laugh from them both. Dasante said, "There you go. Clarity." He stood and brushed his pants off. "Now get off your butt and gather a crowd for me. Tonight, after work, you can come over and take a look at it."

"You got it, D."

The evening had been a good one. It was busy enough that she didn't have much time to think, brought healthy tips, and had Zeb's beaming face behind the bar as he served and talked and generally stayed in motion from the first customers to the last. When she left, he was smoking his pipe across from the elderly wizard, and she was fairly sure their animated discussion was a rehash of the most recent game night.

Cali shook her head and held the door for Fyre. She'd never been to Dasante's home so she had to rely on the mapping software on her phone. It led her generally north and east. Her current abode was more directly east. It took a half-hour of walking before she began to see buildings that looked like they might be apartments and another ten minutes to find the right one. It was in a block of tall buildings with stairs that led to entrances on the second floor. She guessed there were probably two units on each of the three living levels, plus storage on the ground floor.

The front door buzzed to allow her to enter in response to her text to Dasante. She climbed the stairs to the top and found two doors. The one on the right was open, and her friend stood inside it, eating a sandwich. Beside it was a closed door with a small *for rent* sign hanging from the knocker. He took the last bite, chewed quickly, and swallowed, then grinned. "You made it. Good." He gestured to the other apartment. "I have the key."

She looked into his apartment as he stepped aside. A short hallway seemed to lead into a combo living-dining area, and she saw a door beyond that. He was back after a brief moment and let her into the other unit. It was sparsely furnished with only a sofa and coffee table in the main room, a stool near a kitchen counter, and a bed frame in the bedroom. Still, it was several times larger than her room at the boarding house. Plus, she wouldn't have to worry about timing her showers around other people. Fyre jumped on the couch, collapsed onto his side, and seemed quite content.

Cali shook her head with a smile and looked at Dasante. "What's the damage?"

He shrugged. "About two hundred more than what you said Mrs. Jackson charges."

Her eyes widened. *That's totally doable.* "Seriously? Why? Is it haunted?"

With a knowing laugh, he replied, "Like I said, I know the owner."

She folded her arms. "Who is it?"

A look of momentary discomfort flickered across his features and he scratched the back of his neck. She wasn't a particularly insightful analyst of body language, but the sense that he didn't want to answer was unmistakable. After a few seconds, he sighed. "My mom's husband owns the building." He was quick to add, "I pay rent and all, but I also help keep things fixed around here and have a say in who gets places when they're open."

After a moment, she nodded. "Kind of like my arrangement with Sensei Ikehara. I get it." He looked relieved. "Are you a good neighbor? And are pets okay?"

He laughed. "Yeah, one of the other tenants has a dog. Much smaller, though."

A thought entered her brain and once there, she couldn't make it leave. She knelt beside the couch. "Hey, buddy, I have the idea you want to do this." He growled happily and wriggled into the padded fabric. "But I think we have a particular secret that needs to be revealed before we say yes, don't you?"

He opened his eyes and stared at her upside down, then rolled off the edge to land on his feet. His gaze locked on hers, and his head shifted slightly toward Dasante. She turned and said, "Okay, D. Try not to freak out."

He looked from her to Fyre and back again. "Is he, like, going to bite me or something?"

The Draksa gave her one of those looks that conveyed more than words ever could about how unappreciated he was and dispelled the illusion to reveal his true form.

Despite her warning, her friend backpedaled into a wall before his brain caught up with his reflexes. She stepped forward and put her hand on his arm. "It's okay. Really.

He's still the same being, you know, only in a different costume."

Dasante shook his head. "What is he?"

"A Draksa. Part dragon, part lizard, all Atlantean."

"And why do you have him?"

She shrugged. "He kind of adopted me. It's a long story. Anyway, I thought you should probably know about him before you agreed to let us move in next door."

He stared in something resembling awe, and she imagined that she had worn a similar expression the first time she'd seen Fyre. "Can I touch him?"

She looked at the Draksa. "Fyre?" He bobbed his head and pushed against Dasante's hand as it ran down his flank. They stayed like that for several minutes before her friend pushed to his feet.

"So, are you in?"

"Just like that?"

He nodded. "Just like that."

"Then we're in."

A broad smile broke out on his face. "Fantastic. He'd better not snore, though. I need my beauty sleep."

Cali groaned and slapped him gently on the back of the head. "Trust me, there's no amount of rest that's gonna fix your face."

He laughed. "I can already see that this will work out great."

CHAPTER SIXTEEN

Saturdays were always exhausting, even when she wasn't moving out of one place and into another. She was at the dojo especially early to make sure it was ready because Ikehara had begun to sneak in a little earlier each day for their sessions to give her more instruction. Cali guessed that he thought he was fooling her from the small smiles she sometimes caught on his face. His extra effort deserved the same from her. *At this rate, though, we'll eventually start our training days at midnight.*

After battering her best efforts at defending with her sticks against his jo staff, he'd had her put them together to fight with matching weapons. That had gone even less well. His teaching style was predominately to explain and then demand mastery, which wasn't a leap she could always make perfectly. Practice, he said, was to help her get there faster by learning from her mistakes. Her skills had markedly improved, but the training always pointed out that she had considerable room to grow.

Afterward, her aching hands and body had made it

through a normal class, followed by connecting her old and new places with a portal so she could shovel things from one to the other. She planned to let Mrs Jackson know she was gone only after the fact and would leave her an extra month of rent to cover finding a replacement tenant. That plus her security deposit would give the woman more than enough time. Both she and Fyre were excited to move into a bigger apartment, and he'd said he thought living next to Dasante would be fun.

That had kept her busy until the moment she had to leave for work and portaled to the Tavern basement. Nine hours of customer service later, she found herself out on the street behind the Dragons, where she breathed in the night air gratefully and embraced her first occasion of relative peace that day. *Damn, I hate Saturday nights.*

The relaxing interlude was shattered by the appearance of a portal about ten feet from her. She was already backing away when five virtually identical men in hoodies, dark braids, dirty jeans, and angry expressions stepped through. Each held a weapon—three for crushing and the other two for cutting or stabbing, all of them close-range choices. The first said, "There she is," and surged into the attack.

Of all the nights to leave Fyre at the apartment, this is the one we choose. He'd wanted to stay in the apartment and learn the sounds of the new place. The second thing to echo in her mind was an internal scream. *Run, stupid!*

She snapped into motion and pounded down the alley that ran behind the Drunken Dragons. It was late enough that when she turned onto the street that led toward the Quarter, there were few people around. That would change as she got closer and maybe she could lose them in the crowd. If it had been two on one or even three on one, she might have taken her chances with them. But five was too many for comfort.

As it turned out, that handful was only there to chase her to the hunters. Another two foes appeared out of nowhere, which forced her to turn aside and run toward a group of buildings she didn't recognize. Her pursuers hooted and hollered as they chased her like baying hounds would have done. Cali had a split second to decide whether to cut to the left, cut to the right, or sprint to the building ahead. She chose the last option and decided that if she could make it through the partially open door and yank it closed, she'd have enough time to summon a portal and get the hell out of there.

She wedged her body into the opening, pushed against the chain that permitted only a small gap, and had the presence of mind to thank fate for not making her the voluptuous bombshell she'd occasionally wished to be. Once inside, she dragged it closed and leaned against it with a sigh of relief. After only a second, her brain yelled a warning. *Move, Cali. They might have another doorway.* She raised her arms and moved them in the correct pattern to summon the travel circle, willing it into existence with her magic. A faint outline appeared in the air like the line of illumination left behind by a child's sparkler.

Then, for no reason at all, it vanished. She frowned and cast the spell again as she focused more intently to bring it into being. This one dissipated before it had even begun. She cursed, dropped into a crouch, and activated the flashlight on her phone to survey the location. *Add night vision to the list of spells I need to learn.* A dark laugh emanated from somewhere nearby and the voice that followed it was equally grave. "There is no need for that, little girl. We have all the light that's required." A series of electrical snaps accompanied his words and florescent lights above came to life. They revealed that she was in the shell of a building. It had originally had three floors, but the top two had apparently collapsed and left large holes except around the edges. The debris had been pushed to the side fairly recently, judging by the marks in the dust and dirt, to create an open space in the center of the main floor.

In the middle of that area stood an imposing man with dark skin and an inky mustache and beard, the latter braided and neatly styled. Muscles rippled under his tight black t-shirt, and he wore matching tactical-looking pants and boots beneath it. He rolled his neck as she studied him and smiled, displaying white teeth. "It's about time you got here. I was getting bored waiting for you." The realization that she'd been herded to this location washed over her, and she sighed loudly.

"You should have sent an invitation. Or, you know, texted me." She walked carefully forward, not wanting to spur him to action. *Damn, I wish Fyre was here. I seriously need to learn that whole telepathy thing. One more item for the list.* "So, I'll go out on a limb here. You're Atlantean?"

He nodded. "Your city is quite nice, though. Once it belongs to us, I might decide to stay above the waves for a while. The people here are weak, but they could provide interesting…diversions." She had no idea what he imagined as he looked off into the distance and definitely didn't want to know. Ever.

"So, what's the deal here, then? A quick chat? Because we could have done it over a drink or something." *In a place less conducive to killing me, maybe.*

He uttered that laugh again, this time colored with condescension. "Hardly. Tonight will be your last among the living. You have sixty seconds to prepare yourself." A rustling in the shadows remaining at the periphery of the room preceded the appearance of several more people, all but one in the standard uniform of the Atlantean gang. The final individual was a woman in a simple dress wearing a necklace with arcane symbol charms hanging from it. Her aura of mystical power swamped Cali despite the distance between them.

I bet you're the reason I couldn't portal out of here. You blocked me somehow. Wench. At first glance, she'd thought the woman might be the same one she'd fought in the Shark who'd almost spitted her with a spear, but this was someone different. There was a cruel twist to her lips that the suited woman had lacked.

She spent ten precious seconds searching for a way out, but all the ground floor exits had multiple bodies in front of them. It was frighteningly clear that she'd never be able to get through before her opponent killed her. She looked up, but the roof was flat without even a skylight to crash through dramatically—assuming she managed controlled flight, which was far from certain. The tall windows that filled the walls of the second level seemed like a potential option but given the level of planning that had brought her there, she was sure someone would cast a spell to stop it.

I guess I'll have to kick his ass, then. She rolled her neck in an unconscious imitation of his action and stepped a little closer to him. Why he'd chosen one-on-one rather than letting the overwhelming numbers do the work she didn't know, but at least it suggested the possibility of a way out —assuming the others would let her be after she'd defeated their champion, of course.

Thirty seconds remained, but it only took half that time to catalog her limited options. The charm necklace encircled her throat, but lacking the proper activation word, it was only a fashion accessory. *Moving that to the top of the list, check.* She was never without her bracelets, so she had that going for her, at least. And...that was basically all. *Damn. Not good.* She lifted her phone. "I'll set this over to the side so it doesn't get broken while I kick your ass." Laughter from all around answered her, which was welcome because it meant they didn't notice the nine-one-one text she sent to Detective Barton. There was hardly any chance the police would arrive in time to help, but it was the only backup plan she had.

She returned to the center and stood ready. "All right, meathead, let's do this."

He grinned. "You're not likely to provide much of a challenge, but that doesn't matter. It will still be a pleasure to battle you, and a win is a win." He said something in a language she didn't understand and raised a hand, beckoning her to make the first move.

Okay, Cali, no holding back. It's him or you, and there's a sarcastic dragon waiting at home who needs you to take care of him so failure isn't an option. She surged forward with a shout.

CHAPTER SEVENTEEN

Her attack was a feint, of course. Given that her fighting style was all about responsiveness and using the enemy's own power against them, accepting the invitation to take the offensive was a clear path to disaster. She halted the charge midway as soon as he began to react. His smooth glide to the side gave her room to circle and she did so.

His laugh was irritating, which was no doubt what he intended. "Are you scared, little girl?"

She willed her sticks into existence and the flow of the magical substance over her hands brought a measure of comfort. "Hardly." Her weapons solidified and she twirled them once. "I'm simply not interested in playing your game. I like mine better."

He nodded. "Fair enough." He whirled his arms and struck the top of one fist with the bottom of the other. As he drew them apart, a glowing weapon appeared in the gap and eventually expanding into a classic trident.

Cali groaned. "Could you be any more stereotypical?

From now on, your name is Jason." His face twisted in confusion and she rolled her eyes. "Momoa. You know, the actor? Aquaman? Never mind. I take it back. He's smart, so clearly, you're not him." She stamped a foot toward him but he failed to react. *Damn.* "Are we simply going to stare at each other all night? Maybe you'd prefer rock-paper-scissors? I warn you, I'm really good at it."

The man shrugged carelessly. "You can't beat me with words, little girl. Are they all you have?"

Thank goodness Sensei Ikehara is a non-traditionalist who believes in some direct action. She spent a moment locking away every thought other than her opponent before she waded in and left a deliberate gap in her defenses on her strong right side. He spun the weapon faster than she would have thought possible and stabbed it at her chest. A loud clang accompanied the impact of her right-hand stick against the fork at the end as she rotated counterclockwise and extended the left one in a strike at his temple. He leaned back to escape it and the reach of his longer weapon protected him. She finished the spin with a leap forward to swipe at his head with the right stick, but he circled away to evade.

His trident slashed across at knee height, and she bounded back to dodge it. In the instant she was in the air, he charged and thrust the blunt end at her face. She caught it with her left stick and tried to circle it aside. He disengaged, stabbed forward with the same part of the weapon, and landed a glancing blow in her ribs as she twisted too slowly to avoid it. Panic surged at the contact, but she pushed it away ruthlessly and gathered herself for his follow-up attack.

Instead, he stepped back with a laugh and wove the trident one-handed through a series of moves that demonstrated his speed, dexterity, and arrogant confidence. "Ah, little girl, there's no way you can defeat me. Give up now and I'll make it mostly painless."

She growled, thoroughly annoyed. It was one thing to have to fight for her existence but another to do it against someone whose idea of trash-talk was limited to "little girl." "Listen, chucklehead, you might want to get out of here before we reach the point of no return. We can still go our separate ways."

He shook his head. "It's not over until you breathe your last at my feet."

"That's not very friendly." She set her stance to be sure she was perfectly balanced. "Bring it, scumbag."

Her opponent gave her another infuriating grin and seized the offensive. She backpedaled and smacked the thrusting trident aside each time it sought her heart, waiting for an opportunity to present itself. Her plans were foiled when she stepped on a piece of broken concrete and stumbled. He took advantage of the distraction and skipped forward to land a kick to her stomach that lifted her and hurled her back. She landed in a skid and crumpled around the burning in her core. His laughter filled the space between them and betrayed his advance, and she scrambled to get up and moving before he could reach her.

His trident scraped along her back as she darted away and scored three lines of fire beneath her shoulders. The sudden shock made her eyes water and a part of her brain started to gibber. The rest of it, though, seemed to spring into clarity as if she'd only then accepted the life-or-death nature of the battle. She walled the pain off with caution tape in her head and narrowed her focus. He was clearly stronger and had greater reach. Her current plan wasn't working, so she needed a new one. She jammed the marked portions of her sticks together and willed them to change, and they melded into a seamless jo staff. Before her advanced training with Ikehara, she would never have had the confidence to use the longer weapon in a real fight. He had drilled her on its benefits and challenges and fought her with an array of weapons until her skills with the jo were at a level he deemed acceptable. In general, though, she preferred the variety of options that paired weapons presented. *But when your opponent is wielding a large, multi-pointed stick, not rushing in to get impaled is a wise choice.*

She surged toward him and stabbed it at his throat, hoping that the surprise move would give her an opening. He batted it away with a scowl and spun his weapon in a half-circle before he jabbed it at her legs. She blocked, and he tried to strike her in the face with the hilt. Deftly, she deflected it with the staff and attempted to sneak it in again, but she couldn't penetrate his defenses. He lifted the trident and hammered it down at her, and she raised the weapon to block it. The impact rang through her hands and knocked the jo out of them. By reflex, she reached for it, only to watch the trident sweep down and knock it away.

What the hell am I doing, fighting the way he wants to? She threw two force punches, and they connected with his chest and face and forced him back a step. Unlike in previous battles, though, they didn't appear to deal significant damage. He released the trident with one hand and brushed at where she'd struck him. "That was a cowardly choice, little girl. But thank you." He flexed his muscles and the trident's glow increased, and a blast of energy streaked from the fork as he pointed it at her. She dove to the side to avoid it and rolled up to her feet as she summoned a force shield to intercept the one that followed. The sheer power of it knocked her off balance and she staggered. *Damn. Not cool. Okay, next plan.*

Cali imagined a giant hand in the air. Her force magic channeled into that shape and caught hold of the trident to yank it from the man's grasp. She bared her teeth and hurled it through one of the windows surrounding the second level. The sound of shattering glass brought inordinate pleasure. Her foe blinked at her like he couldn't comprehend what had happened. She gave him the smile she reserved for particularly slow and stupid customers. He clearly understood the message and attacked with a growl.

Now this is my kind of fight. He threw a broad haymaker with his left and she redirected it with an outside-in block and latched onto his wrist. She rotated it downward and wrenched it up behind his back, but he spun and threw an elbow at her head before she could get the joint locked out. Cali swayed to the side to avoid the blow but lost her grip as he drove forward. Her foot lashed out in a kick at his spine, but his speed took him out of range before it could land.

She imagined the force hand again, snagged a piece of stone lying on the floor, and hurled it at him when he turned. A magical bracer appeared on his arm, and he intercepted the projectile with a downward slash that shattered it into rubble. She yelled, "Cut it out," before she could restrain herself and threw more rocks at him. The Atlantean was completely calm as he deflected or destroyed them before they could do any damage.

Her foe seemed to concentrate for a moment, and the glow expanded to cover his fists. He held them up, inviting her to admire them. "You have only to stop running, little girl."

Cali growled her annoyance. "Name-calling is immature. Knock it off." She threw several more pieces of rubble, noticed that her supply was diminishing fast, and cast about for other options. A piece of the second level to her left hung by only four spikes of rebar that projected from the wall and she decided she could probably pull it down if she could get him beneath it. *Of course, he might be able to do that to me with his sparkly hands, too, so that's a problem.* She raced in that direction when her ammunition ran out but stopped before moving under the weakened area. He closed the distance with his fists raised like a boxer to protect himself.

She threw punches but he blocked the magic blows before they struck anything vital. The threat of her imminent demise grew with each step. Casting an illusion to drive him into the trap occurred to her, but a quick glance at the woman in the fancy necklace revealed that she was watching carefully. The sight dredged up a half-memory of a story told by her parents about Atlantean gladiators and how only physical manifestations of arcane power were permitted in ritual combat. An illusion might change the rules the same way her force attack had if this was one of those, and she definitely didn't want the people standing around to join in.

Her adversary reciprocated her strategy and flung a rock at her head, but she ducked and summoned a large shield to deflect the others he threw on his run toward her. She extended her hand and willed her magical weapon to return to her, and it arrived barely in time for her to stop his charge and keep him at a distance. It wouldn't last, though. Her skills weren't enough to deter him while protecting the staff from his grasp if he decided to take it from her. She circled and focused her concentration for a final attack.

Using the technique Emalia had taught her, Cali reached for his mind with hers. She saw the outline again and pushed in but didn't get the series of dots she'd had with her teacher. Instead, she encountered a thick barrier. She frowned and imagined herself moving around him until she found a place that looked less strong. Calmly, she pressed against it, pictured her thrust as a needle, and punched through. It took only a moment to implant fear of a sudden fire attack, and she followed it immediately with an illusion that existed only in his head of a cone of flames that rocketed toward him. He flinched and dodged to the side.

His evasive maneuver placed him under the weakened concrete.

Cali snapped out her force hand and pounded its fist on the stone to shatter it and drop the pieces on her foe. When the rumble faded and the dust settled, he was trapped under a large section and only barely conscious. Blood trickled from his nose and the corner of his mouth, and his eyes stared without focus. She turned a slow circle, ready to engage any of the others who might attack her, but none seemed interested in doing so. When her gaze reached the woman, she stepped forward and nodded. "You have won this battle, Caliste, and have thus advanced to the next level of combat. You have a week to rest, recuperate, and prepare."

"Okay, wait a second. What the hell are you talking about, lady?"

She smiled. "The rules do not require me to explain the many things of which you are ignorant, princess." Syrupy sarcasm dripped from the final word.

Cali had now had enough of the abundant condescension. She scowled. "You people need to get something straight. No one calls me princess, or a little girl, or child, or whatever. You haven't earned the privilege. And unless you want to go a round right now, you'll knock that garbage off."

The woman shook her head, her irritating grin unchanged. "I'd like nothing more, little girl. But it would be breaking the rules for me to attack you. However, if you wish to start something, I am more than happy to oblige." She folded her hands in front of her in the most annoying and superior manner possible.

Cali thought about—really thought about—making her eat her words. A rustle from behind her dispelled the idea quickly, and she strode toward the exit. The man blocking it waited until she stopped eye to eye with him to move out of the way, and she gave him a grin. "We'll settle up for that later, jerk."

He nodded. "Anytime, child."

She suppressed a growl as she exited the building and ran into the darkness to find a place to cast a portal. Sirens were audible nearby, and she texted an all-clear to the Detective so she wouldn't engage the Atlanteans. *Now, I'll have to explain everything that went down here to her. Damn, I hate Saturday nights.*

CHAPTER EIGHTEEN

Tanyith scratched at the collar of his dress shirt, which was annoyingly over-starched. The outfit had been laundered in preparation for his trip to the Stallion Bar, and the place he'd used was apparently really excited about making everything perfectly stiff and creased. Still, based on his own knowledge from the past and Detective Barton's from the present, the expectations for sartorial splendor inside those walls remained high.

The entrance was a block ahead. He'd parked down two more in the opposite direction so no one would connect him with the motorcycle. It was entirely possible tonight's outing would lead to more surveillance, so he needed every ounce of anonymity he could get. It was almost certain that the Zatoras had the place watched at all times. A magical disguise would have been too dangerous, but he had dyed his hair and beard black and put enough product in them to mask their normal shape.

The Stallion Bar had been neutral territory for the

human gangs for far longer than he'd known of its existence. The stories said that one of the gangs opened it as a way to launder money, and when the others arrived to fight, they instead made a deal to keep it running. All the gangs were welcome and any of them were permitted to use its services freely. Over time, those services grew as the number of competing factions diminished. Now, it was primarily a Zatora stronghold, Kendra had said, but the other gangs still maintained a minority ownership interest. She assumed it was a means for the syndicate to keep tabs on the potential competition and he had no reason to doubt her assessment.

A bouncer stood at the entry door, but a twenty-dollar bill and the words, "Room at the bar?" got him inside. Barton had pressed an informant or two to learn that particular piece of information. She'd also discovered that he had to slip the bartender another bill before he'd get the reserved sign moved away from in front of an empty chair, which was a method of identifying those who didn't belong. There was no way to know each member of every gang, so the rituals kept the uninitiated at arm's length.

The transaction went smoothly, and he ordered rye on the rocks and earned a nod of approval from the man behind the bar. Tanyith's dark suit was quite similar to those worn by the wait staff, but his black shirt and long blue tie differed from their white shirts and ebony bow ties. When the drink arrived, he sipped it and absorbed the atmosphere. The main restaurant took up most of the space, filled with four tables in the middle and booths on either side. They were occupied by well-dressed men and better-dressed women, all of whom appeared to be enjoying an evening out. *Date night for the gangster crowd.* Tanyith chuckled inwardly.

The bar, on the other hand, was entirely populated by solo men in dark suits who possessed the solid looks of people who worked hard for a living. Very likely, their careers were a little different than those holding down chairs at other restaurant bars—shooters instead of stock-brokers and numbers runners instead of accountants—but the feel was the same. There was a shared camaraderie among the dateless assuaging their sorrows with alcohol.

He finished his first drink and ordered the next. When the bartender returned, Tanyith asked, "Hey, have you worked here long?"

The man had the build of an aging high school quarter-back, with broad shoulders and arm muscles that pushed against the fabric of his suit. His hair was starting to thin visibly, despite the careful part that swept it all over to one side. He sported an impressive brown mustache, and he toyed with it while he worked. His voice was smooth and his tone professional but guarded. "Sure, about four years or so and full-time for the last two. Are you new in town?"

He shrugged. "I was away for a while. Things changed in the meantime. I'm new here, though. A friend of mine told me it was a good place to meet important people. Is that true?"

The bartender chuckled. "Well, you met me. What do you think?" He turned and headed to another customer.

Tanyith sighed. *Basically what I expected, but damn, I don't have the time to invest to build credibility here.* He thought for a few moments about what he might do and swept his gaze over the dining room before he froze in astonishment. Right there, across the expanse of tables from him and seated in a booth with a beautiful woman at his side was Dray, one of the people from his time with the Atlantean gang whom Sienna had said was missing. *What the hell is he doing here?* There were only two options he could see. First, he was part of a rival group in town and was undercover. But the Dray that he remembered wasn't really into that kind of thing, nor was he equipped for it. The other option was equally concerning. Could his old friend have joined one of the human factions?

If he hadn't seen the man's face clearly, he wouldn't have recognized him. The facial hair he remembered was gone, and his clean-shaven features were sharper than they had been before. He looked like he'd lost a dozen pounds, at least, and had seriously cleaned up his act. His suit cost easily twice what his own had, by the looks of it, and the jewelry on the woman he was with would probably have paid Tanyith's rent for six months or so. His mind was vapor-locked until the moment when Dray excused himself and headed to the back of the dining room and toward where Tanyith presumed the restrooms were. He left a large tip on the bar and made his move.

The woman seemed surprised when he stopped in front of the table. She was a redhead with darker curls than Cali's and big green eyes in a perfectly made-up face. He imagined there were freckles beneath the makeup, and she appeared younger than she had from across the room— early twenties, tops, he guessed. *Dray is robbing the cradle. I should get Kendra in here to arrest him.* She didn't seem concerned by his presence and merely looked doubtfully at him and asked, "Do I know you?"

He gave his most disarming smile. "Not yet, but we have a friend in common. Your date and I go way back. Sorry for being weird and coming over like this, but I was really shocked to see him."

"Okay." The word held doubt. "Maybe you should wait for him to return, then. Back wherever you came from."

"I'll do exactly that." He nodded reassuringly. "I only wanted to ask what kind of wine you both liked so I can send some over as a surprise."

Her guard didn't drop but her suspicion lessened a touch. "Cabernet."

"Thanks. Enjoy your evening." He turned and headed to the bar to place the order. The whole exercise had been a ruse to get a better look at her, and it was a relief that the woman hadn't made a scene. He was out the cost of a bottle but he'd gained a little data. *That will probably turn out to be useless.* He sighed. *This investigation gig is for the birds.*

He was a block away on his idling bike, the helmet protecting his anonymity, when the couple exited the restaurant and strolled to a car. Dray helped the woman in and slid behind the wheel, and Tanyith trailed as far back as he could without losing sight of them. The dark sedan pulled over to the curb in front of an apartment building and the woman got out, then leaned through the open window to say something. She stood with a smile and gave a wave as she turned to head inside the ornate door atop a short flight of steps. He'd imagined the two of them finishing the night together so was surprised when Dray drove toward the Quarter rather than finding a parking space.

Twenty minutes later, he was on foot behind his old friend, weaving through the tourists on Bourbon Street. Fortunately, Sunday nights weren't quite as crazy as the weekend, so he had a reasonably easy time keeping tabs on the other man. It also made it more likely that he'd see an attack before it reached him. After the text from Cali detailing her adventures the night before, he'd been suspicious of everyone and everything.

His quarry turned into a tourist trap nightspot and he followed with a groan. On the upside, there was no bouncer waiting to accept more of his dwindling cash supply. On the downside, it was full of people dancing, drinking, and generally getting in the way of his pursuit. Dray's dark hair and clothes were tinted by the island-themed neon signs as he pushed through the room, and Tanyith trailed as closely as he dared. His quarry's objective seemed to be a closed door at the back of the space, this one with a bored man standing beside it. The guard stifled a yawn as they drew closer.

Dray exchanged words with him and the guy nodded. Tanyith cursed inwardly as his friend stepped through. There was no chance he could bluff his way past the guard, and any magical distraction he might use would risk spooking the crowd and blowing the whole thing. Loud voices caught his attention from the left as one man shoved another, and he smothered the grin that the scene inspired. *You can never go wrong when you count on drunk people getting into arguments.* At the next push, he fired a force blast to knock the recipient of the shove down. There were more shouts as the one who'd been pushed bounced up from the floor and went after the confused attacker.

He circled around the edge while he kept one eye on the fracas and the other on the guard. Finally, the man couldn't ignore the situation any longer and he strode in to break it up. Tanyith tossed up a hasty illusion to hide his passage through the door and closed it quietly behind him. This part of the club was unexpectedly elegant. The hallway he was in had been painted a rich brown and was lit with wall sconces to create a soft, calming atmosphere. It led in only one direction, so he followed it and walked softly to keep the noise of his shoes on the off-white tile floor as subdued as possible. A corner lay ahead, and he put his back against the wall before it and stuck his head around as quickly and stealthily as he was able.

A very large man stood in the center of the hallway. He smiled and nodded. "I've been asked to escort you the rest of the way." He looked as if he wouldn't mind at all if he had to enforce that request with violence.

Tanyith sighed. *It's possible that I'm not cut out for investigative work.*

He was reintroduced to his friend when he was ushered into a makeshift office in what he guessed had been a storeroom in the recent past. A beat-up desk was inside, and a couple of chairs were set before it. The other man sat in one of them and nodded at his entrance. "Tanyith. We've heard about you and assumed you'd pop up on the radar. I'm Ray." Up close, it was clear that not only had he lost fat, but he'd also gained muscle. His old friend had the trappings of a fighter, right down to the short crewcut that would prevent an enemy from grabbing his hair. The eyes still remembered mischief, but they, too, seemed harder.

He raised an eyebrow. "Ray, is it?"

"It is," he responded with a thin smile. A glance at the bouncer dispatched him from the room. As the door closed behind him, Dray gave the old signal for surveillance, and Tanyith's brow furrowed. *Okay, what the hell is going on here?*

"So, my people saw you following me from the Stallion. I can only assume you're one of us and you're sick of the magicals who are taking over the town." His jaw threatened to fall open in shock but he caught it before it made it too far.

"Uh...yeah, Ray. Exactly. How did you know?"

The man shrugged and leaned back in the office-style chair. It creaked. "The Stallion tends to draw a certain type. And you knew the right things to say and do, so you must be a friend of one of us." His gaze shifted from casual to intense. "What is it you need?"

He took the look to mean that he needed to tread carefully. "Okay, here's the deal. I'm looking for a guy. My...uh, boss needs to speak to him. Something about an old debt."

Dray-Ray grinned. "There's a fair amount of that whole past coming back to life stuff going around lately. Maybe it's the New Orleans magic, right?" He chuckled. "So, who is it?"

"Aiden Walsh."

His once-friend frowned. "I haven't seen or heard from

that guy in, like, half a year, I think. Why the sudden interest?"

Tanyith shrugged. "I'm only the messenger here. I don't know and don't care. But it's my ass if I don't find him, so anything you have to point me in the right direction would be much appreciated."

The other man scratched the side of his face. "Yeah, I can dig something up. What are you offering for it?" Another hand signal followed, this time for "deal."

He frowned, tried to parse the message, but failed. "I don't know. What do you want?"

Ray nodded. "I could use a deniable. There's someone who owes us money who won't pay up. Maybe you can make him see the light. If you get pinched, don't even think of mentioning us or your hours in jail will be short and fatally violent."

Damn. It might have been better to stay in prison. The very thought made him shudder inside, and he grasped the arms of his chair to steady himself. "If that's the price, I'll pay it." *At this rate, I'll have too much work going on to actually land a real job.*

The other man rose and spoke in a businesslike tone. "Good. Your escort will help you find your way out of the club and give you the details. Get the job done, and we'll talk about the information you want." Tanyith gripped his extended hand while Dray continued to speak. "Do this right and maybe there's a place for you with us. Do it wrong, and...well, finding the guy you're looking for will be the least of your troubles."

He looked into the familiar eyes and saw truth in them. The door opened without any action on either of their parts, confirming that someone was listening, watching, or both. Whatever was going on, his simple search for the disappearing boyfriend had become something much more serious. *And, judging by the look in Dray's eyes, much more dangerous.*

CHAPTER NINETEEN

Tanyith sat at the counter of a chain coffee shop and stared out the window. He'd done a quick check-in with Detective Barton first thing at the start of the business day and discovered she was not a morning person. Still, she'd given him the extra information required to decide whether or not to do the job for Dray—*and damn it, I don't care what he's calling himself, he's Dray to me*—and also where to find the guy.

Fortunately for him, James Crain was a lowlife, even among the losers that made up some of the least palatable human gangs. The rap sheet Barton had called up was replete with petty crimes of every kind, but the offense that was really bothersome was a chain of drug arrests near schools. They'd never made the charges stick and the more junior people inevitably took the fall, but everything pointed to him as an overseer, if not a particularly trusted or elevated one.

The information he'd obtained from the brute at the club had simply provided a name and an address. When he asked how much his target owed, the giant man had laughed and said in his ridiculously deep voice, "He'll know." Tanyith had nodded and made his exit, assuming that either the man wasn't willing to share because he was a jerk or didn't know because he was an idiot. He had resigned himself to handling it without any more assistance from Dray's people.

Across the street was a location that Barton said Crain tended to frequent for late breakfasts. He checked the photo on his phone for at least the fifteenth time since she'd sent it to him. It was a booking shot of a man with a flat-top haircut, long sideburns, and a neck tattoo of some calligraphic script that he couldn't make out. He'd considered blowing the picture up but decided the risk of becoming dumber by reading whatever the chucklehead chose to put indelibly in his skin was too damn high. His hair was on the border of black and brown, and his features were sharp. He looked too skinny, a common problem for those who dabbled with the drugs they sold.

He forced himself to stay seated when Crain appeared across the street, walking in cadence with another man. Tanyith estimated the second one was about five-seven, a full six inches shorter than his quarry. They both wore white basketball jerseys celebrating the Pelicans. Others in his group had been fans, but team sports generally didn't appeal to him. He hadn't heard anything about them since his return but presumed they were still around. Snatching his coffee, he headed out the door and turned in the same direction in which the duo traveled.

They ate as they walked, wolfing sandwiches held in paper. The sight made his stomach rumble. He'd avoided food in favor of fretting about what Barton might reveal, and even though he was fully confident that Crain would deserve whatever he got, eating before a probable fight hadn't seemed like a good idea. He regretted it now, but there was no time to stop for something. He was fairly sure he knew their destination, but it was always possible he might be wrong.

Sadly, he turned out to be right. They turned into an alley a couple of blocks away from a park notorious for being a hangout for high schoolers skipping school. It had basketball courts and some skateboarding rails and curves but was also home to small groups of people who hung out and looked for trouble. Marked police cars drove past at intervals, but those present in the space had serious skills in fading away and returning after the trouble had passed. Tanyith expected that they had lookouts posted but knew that if the police really cared, they'd arrive in plainclothes and on foot. No, it was a mutual agreement situation—don't get out of hand and we won't work too hard to catch you.

He was fine with that choice, but the drug angle turned it on its head. In general, he couldn't bring himself to care too much about what competent adults did as long as they didn't hurt anyone else, but trying to manipulate under-eighteens into a dependency was an entirely different story. Even if the kids themselves would tell him they made their own choices and he should go to hell, it didn't matter. His personal ethics were clear where non-adults were concerned.

So he's enough of a scumbag that other scumbags want him dealt with. That's impressive, really. He considered that for a second and laughed. *I guess that describes Cali and I at the moment too, so we have that going for us.* He watched for almost an hour and moved to a couple of different positions so as to not attract attention and thought he found the right plan. The best time to strike would be between visits from the folks at the bottom of the chain who collected and distributed. They seemed to report in at ten-minute intervals, either to drop cash off or to get permission or something. He didn't know and didn't think he needed to.

Tanyith circled and chose a position a half-block away and across the street. He was about to make a move when a black-and-white rolled through and upset the entire arrangement. It took another forty minutes before things had resumed a predictable pattern again, and he feared that the police would follow hour intervals, so he needed to get it done. When he had moved from position to position, he had left homemade smoke bombs in several trashcans, all awaiting a signal from the car starter remote in his pocket. They'd been a very useful part of his toolkit in the past. He'd been beyond happy to discover that they still worked when he'd retrieved them from the apartment wall they'd been hidden in a year and a half earlier.

They detonated in a pattern that would drive people away from his targets, and he was already in motion as the panic began. His gaze was locked on them as he rushed forward, and the smaller one flinched when he detected him and realized what was happening. He did the good subordinate thing and drew a gun while his partner ran. Tanyith growled and cursed, not wanting to use his magic for fear he might be called on it later if anyone saw him. If he wanted to get information from a human group, being outed could be problematic. He twitched his fingers as he started to run in a zig zag and hoped for the best. The rock he'd seen hurtled up from the ground into the man's hand like it had been thrown and the pistol flew away.

Tanyith reached the thug while he was still processing the sudden disarming, and he snapped an elbow into his face as he passed. His foe fell with a cracking sound onto the hard surface of the alley, and he took a hasty look over his shoulder to ensure it had been something non-vital that had broken. The hoodlum wouldn't use his arm for a while by the look of things, but the injuries didn't appear life-threatening. He swiveled his head forward as the tail of the white jersey whipped around the corner and out of sight.

Dammit, faster. He increased his speed, already panting from the exertion. His time in prison hadn't been like the movies, where you went in flabby and came out as hard as stone. Trevilsom had torn everything away and his body seemed to consume itself to keep him alive and sane. He still didn't know how he'd managed to survive it, but the upshot was that he wasn't in anything near the best shape of his life. All he needed now was this one break. Thereafter, he promised himself, he would not only work harder at getting healthy, but he'd also think of ways to make the criminals come to him, rather than the other way around.

A little luck did come into play when he reached the main street. The man was still in sight, running away from the park, which was what he'd hoped the dealer would do. He pushed his burning legs to keep moving and stayed on his tail. He'd have much preferred taking to the roofs and following him from there, but he had to preserve his cover.

The chance that this guy would talk his way into a meeting with Dray's gang was remote, but it was non-zero. If it were only his safety on the line, he might have done it, but with his connection to the tavern known by too many people, he'd risk Cali and Zeb too.

The crook did something completely unexpected and darted into a door set in the side of one of the buildings. Nothing he'd received suggested that he had connections here. *Damn, damn, damn.* The only option was to follow him in, and he thrust against the door with a blast of force leading his shoulder and powered through the weak lock. A staircase ascended in front of him and a hallway led to the right. The back part of his brain processed the sound he'd heard a moment before and ordered him upward. He dashed up the steps, caught sight of his prey again, and followed him around the spiraled stairs until they reached the roof.

The man bolted to the side. Tanyith had to hold back his first instinct, which was to smack him with a force blast and put his face in the gravel. The possibility that he'd fall into the street was too high and there could still be someone watching. He drew on all his speed as Crain leapt over the edge and made it cleanly across the single-lane gap between buildings. His pursuer made the jump immediately after, and when the man ran between some HVAC equipment that shielded him from other eyes, he blasted his feet with a burst of magical force. The fugitive tripped and fell, skidding and screaming. Tanyith slowed and worked on catching his breath as he covered the distance between them and kicked the man's legs out from under him when he tried to rise.

"You. Stay. Down." He panted and fought to calm his breathing. The man on his back below him looked more worn than the one in the picture and the cuts on his face from the gravel changed the shading somewhat, but it was clearly still the same guy. "James Crain. Some people are mad at you." The man's hand began to creep toward his body, and he tapped him with the toe of his boot. "Don't even think about it. If I have any worry that you're going for a weapon, all the ribs on this side will be broken before you can clear it. You and I both know you're not that good."

Sure, it was a petty taunt. He deserves it for making me run. Bastard. "Okay, so you're probably wondering why I'm here. Is that right? Are you capable of speech, man? Say something."

Crain dabbed at the blood on his lip with his fingers and looked at it, then replied, "Yeah. I can talk. I assume you're trying to take my territory."

He shook his head. "Nope, wrong. But that's good, right? Now you can relax. I'm here because you owe some people something. I'm sure you know which people, and I'm sure you know what you owe them. The kind of people who would send someone like me to get the payment with orders that failing to do so means failing to continue breathing. Does that sound familiar?"

"Yeah. I get it." He blanched and nodded. "But I don't have it on me."

Tanyith shrugged. He'd expected as much. "That's fine. You can take me to where it is."

The man looked at him like he was crazy. "It's across town."

"Not a problem. I'll even pay for the ride. But be aware that if you try anything—literally any single thing—I have been given the option to end this the other way and I won't hesitate to do so." He hadn't, actually, and he wouldn't, but the loser on the ground didn't need to know that. "Now, get up slowly and turn your pockets out one at a time."

He collected a knife and a street-special holdout pistol that he removed the ammunition from and smashed on the roof until it was inoperative. Satisfied that his captive was now weaponless, he marched him down to the road and called a car. When the driver tried to talk, Tanyith explained that his friend had a migraine and he was taking him home to recover, but that noise was a problem. The remainder of the trip passed in blessed silence.

They were dropped off in an old neighborhood with small houses featuring tiny patches of green at the front and back. It was midday, so they received some strange looks, and the situation grew weirder when he discovered that the man's grandmother was in the house. She slept in the living room, and they crept quietly past and ascended to the attic. Once there, the guy sighed. "I knew they would demand it but I didn't want to give it up, you know? Once I got it for them, I decided I wanted to keep it."

Tanyith shook his head. "I have no idea and what's more, I don't care. Hand it over." Crain opened a knee-high box and rummaged in the bottom to withdraw a thick blue cloth. He unfolded it carefully and suddenly stabbed it at him. Tanyith saw a flash of silver as he backpedaled to avoid whatever it was, then drove forward, leading with his fists when it missed. His left connected with the other man's temple, and his right uppercut caught him in the jaw. Crain splayed awkwardly, unconscious on the floor. "Dammit. You're an idiot, you know that?" He picked up the sharp piece of metal and wrapped it in the cloth once again. His fingers traced the etchings absently as he did so.

Leaving the man where he was, he snuck out of the house and called another ride. He had a delivery to make, which would hopefully allow him to get back to his actual task. *Life outside sure is complicated.*

CHAPTER TWENTY

Usha had sat in the dark for half an hour while she contemplated how best to report the enforcer's failure to the Empress. On the one hand, it wasn't her failure. It was his. But on the other, since he was more or less in her direct line of authority now, she shared in it. That was one of many reasons her ruler limited her own enforcers to those who had repeatedly proven their superiority in the trials so they would be unlikely to reflect badly upon her. The threat of death for defeat was an added incentive not to damage her image.

Water sounds emanated from hidden speakers, soothing some of the mounting stress. She didn't fear punishment from her superior. What horrified her was the idea that the other woman would believe she was inadequate in some way. In any way. While she had her own dreams and goals, they only existed within the boundaries of the Empress's desires. It had been she who had dispatched Usha to New Orleans with the mandate to ready the city for occupation. And it had been she who had seen something special in the woman who'd fought brutally through a series of opponents to earn the opportunity to pledge her life to her. She'd had to do so in one of the rare public trials, lacking the appropriate bloodline or patrons to enter the Empress's presence in any other fashion.

Her soul shivered at the idea of disappointing the woman she served. It would be a failure she would literally not be able to live with.

A chime indicated that she had only five minutes remaining before she was to be available to commune. She stood and smoothed her jade-green dress and checked in a small hand mirror from the desk to ensure that her hair was properly styled and accessorized. A net over her braids held sparkling gems and bright pieces of coral. They matched the heavy necklace at her throat and the bracelets on her wrists. She had even chosen her best perfume, although as far as she knew, the communication did not include senses other than sight and sound.

She sighed. *As far as I know. That's the key to everything. I need to know more and I am surrounded by people with more muscle than mind.* She shook her head. *I'll have to risk giving Danna more tasks.* She imagined that the relationship she had with the Empress was replicated between her and her second, with Usha in the superior role. It made her not want to endanger the other woman unnecessarily, which was something she hoped her own ruler felt about her.

Another chime signaled one minute. She cast the spell to unlatch the door, entered the lightless room, and pulled it shut behind her. It was vision and soundproof until the sphere in the basin in the front began to glow and the vapor appeared. She waited quietly and the sounds of crashing waves and whale song that always accompanied commune washed over her. One by one, she let her barriers fall and allowed herself to become part of that symphony for a time.

But when the vapors began to move, she snapped back to attention with complete focus. The face of her ruler materialized before her, simultaneously solid and ghostly. She bowed deeply. "Empress."

The other woman's voice was smooth, low, and resonant. She felt it as much as heard it. "My servant. What news?"

Usha had decided to start with the positives. "We are increasing our customer base for the magical drug, which we have called Zarcanum. My people expect that we will have more demand than supply for the next month or so, at least."

The Empress nodded. "Well done. That is ahead of schedule, is it not?"

She was always amazed at her ruler's ability to keep so many details close to hand. "Yes, it is. And all signs point to that continuing." She received a nod and pressed on. "The drug to addict the humans is almost ready. It is too often fatal, so we are working on a less potent dose."

"But keeping the original formula as well, no doubt? Because such things can be quite useful."

Usha nodded. "Yes, Empress. We have a supply in case we need to create an epidemic."

"Or eliminate a particular target. Indeed. Well done, my servant."

She blushed with pride and forced her voice to seriousness. "Territory expansion is not going as well. The intervention of the dwarf and his minions has complicated the situation. However, my people are working to deal with that problem as we speak."

"Have the enforcers I sent been useful?"

She didn't sigh or allow her face to react with anything other than a smile. "They have been, Empress. One has already attempted to eliminate the girl who broke in here. Due to the vagaries of chance, I'm told, that battle did not end in our favor."

"Is he still alive?"

"He is, Empress, and ready to make partial amends with the next attempt. He recognizes and regrets his failure."

The other woman chuckled. "What penance did you assign him?"

Usha grinned. "Restroom monitor for the club."

Her ruler broke out into laughter. "Truly, you possess a wicked streak, my servant. He must find that entirely humiliating, given all that he has accomplished."

She nodded. "Yes, Empress. He does. However, I set the duration for only ten days. I don't wish to break him, only twist him."

Her superior nodded and tapped her chin with a long finger. The nail was metallic silver, and Usha had often wondered if it was paint or a weapon. "Make it fourteen days. Let him simmer."

"Yes, Empress." she bowed her head. "Your will is my desire."

"What of the other one?"

She knew the woman referred to the other troublemaker, Tanyith. "He has been seen in a variety of places, and we believe we have his movements tracked well enough to intervene. I will send the other enforcer to handle it."

The Empress nodded. "Impress upon him the consequences of failure. Remind him that I am watching."

Usha swallowed hard. That was a phrase with a double meaning, clearly intended both for him and for her. She whispered, "Yes, Empress."

The other woman smiled. "With you, I am well pleased. See that you stay ahead of schedule." Without anything further, the vapors dissipated and Usha stumbled out of the room, breathing like she'd actually run a race. There was something deeply terrifying and yet immensely pleasurable about being in the woman's presence. She felt it more intensely each time they communed. A small part of her mind worried that she was being magicked, but the rest accepted whatever the connection might cost as the price of the future she wanted.

She retrieved her phone from the locked desk and sent several texts, then sat in the expensive and comfortable chair to await her subordinates.

Danna was the first to arrive. She was dressed entirely in black, and a frown defined her face. She'd taken the enforcer's failure personally, which was hierarchically appropriate, but it was no more her fault than it was Usha's. *When your Empress gives you a tool, it is not your failure if the tool is inadequate to what should have been a simple task.*

And that was the key. *It should have been simple.* They'd underestimated the girl, clearly. It was easy to attribute it to the blood running through her veins, but that was a far too simplistic answer. They hadn't given her enough respect, from Usha on down, and it had resulted in a failure. But not a determining one. She gestured for the woman to take the chair across from her.

The light-skinned blonde enforcer was the next to enter. She beckoned him forward and he stood at the corner of the desk where both women could see him. His face was neutral and emotionless, as befitted his role. She tilted her chin at him. "So. Your brother failed."

The man nodded. "He did."

"What are your thoughts on that?"

He moved his hands behind his back and presumably clasped them there. "The intelligence we had at the time suggested that the strategy should have worked. Clearly, she is more than we thought. However, he cannot be held blameless. It is his obligation to adapt and succeed and in this, he failed."

She turned to Danna. "And your thoughts?"

The woman shrugged. "Failure at multiple levels. But we can learn from it and do better on the next go-round. She will have the right to additional support, as will we, so it will be a greater challenge to find the perfect moment." A frown flickered across her face. "Unless we wish to explain things to her."

Usha shook her head. "No. Not now and potentially not ever. That would create many, many more problems for us. We will simply have to ensure that the rules are followed on both sides. Next time, two on two." Her second in command nodded to acknowledge the decision, and Usha turned to the enforcer.

"So. Fortunately, we don't have to limit ourselves at all where Tanyith is concerned. Take whoever you think you need and kill him. If there is anyone with him, they're fair game unless it's the girl." She stared hard into his eyes. "Understand what I'm saying. If you touch one hair on that girl's head for any reason other than by my direct command, you and your brother will beg to die for days before I set you free to live the rest of your life without eyes, fingers, or a tongue."

He didn't react except for a tightening at the corners of his eyes. He nodded. "I understand. My purpose is to serve. I will kill the man and I will not touch Leblanc."

"Excellent. Leave." He obeyed and closed the door softly behind him. She turned to Danna with a smile. "Too strong?"

Her second in command shook her head. "Absolutely not. Enforcers tend to favor emotion over reason at times. It is good to remind them of the need for a balance of both."

Usha sighed. "I wish more of my people approached your level of wisdom and ability. But since they don't, I will have to ask more of you than I'd prefer to."

Danna nodded. "I assumed that would be the case after the setback with Caliste. Have no worries. I'm capable of whatever you need and willing to do whatever you wish." The words warmed her soul. Leadership could be lonely, and she was lucky to have such a dedicated subordinate. In another life, they'd be friends. In this one, their power relationship would always restrict true connection. *Well, maybe one day when this is all over and we're both retired, that could change.* She laughed inwardly. *Quite a dream.*

"Excellent. Together, we'll keep things on track and on schedule."

"What would you like me to do first?"

She smiled. "We need to push harder on distributing the Zarcanum."

Danna's expression matched her own. "As it happens, I have some thoughts on that."

CHAPTER TWENTY-ONE

The sensation of Fyre's cold nose against her bare leg hadn't been an improvement over the wake-up app on her phone, even if the most recent song Dasante had elected was a polka from Weird Al Yankovic that would be in her mind for at least another week. The Draksa had been insistent, however, and they'd jogged around the block to warm up before the sun appeared.

Although the new apartment building had a strip of grass in the back, they'd scouted and found a reasonable-sized area a couple of streets away. While they would maintain overlapping veils while they trained together and Fyre would retain his dog disguise as a backup, it would certainly look weird if a Rottweiler suddenly gained the ability to breathe frost. It wasn't clear what the area had been before whatever had occupied it was demolished, but it was now a large, uneven patch of dirt and grass.

She collected a few fist-sized stones and a couple of discarded Coke bottles and placed them on a small mound at one end. Pointing to it, she explained, "That's our target.

Let's imagine that he's all the *Terminator* villains rolled together." The way the Draksa looked at her conveyed his scorn. "Uh, right, sure, you haven't seen the movies because you're a dragon lizard." *Or because you have no taste, more like.* She laughed inwardly. "Okay, virtually unbreakable Kilomea." He nodded, that image clearly much more resonant.

They moved to the far end of the field and she said, "All right, this is your time to shine."

He sounded focused, his usual mirth and-or sarcasm absent. "Do you want to go in side by side or do it close-up and ranged?"

She thought about it for a second, but his previous observations about her nature held true. Plus, she couldn't be sure her aim was good enough to avoid hitting him and she wouldn't feel right hiding in the back. "We do it together."

"Okay." He nodded. "I'll go to the right and you go to the left, which keeps your dominant hand toward him. We'll assume my frost doesn't stop him, but you'll have to wait until it passes to engage or you'll get caught. We can practice that until our timing's perfect."

"Got it." Strangely, it didn't feel odd at all taking strategy lessons from Fyre. They ran in to attack half a dozen times while she gained a sense of his speed before he began to vary the tactics and made her adapt. After fifteen attempts, she was tired but confident and competent in the approach. She called a break to rest and checked her phone, happy to discover it hadn't taken more time than she'd expected. There was still an hour and a half before she had to be at the dojo, and even though it took a little longer to get there from the new apartment, the timing looked good.

She reached out absently and patted Fyre on the back. "Life's weird these days, my friend."

He leaned toward her a little but continued to look off into the distance. "Why?"

Cali shrugged. "Mysteries all over, right? What's up with the Zatoras? What's up with the Atlanteans? Why did my parents leave me a key to a place I can't find, a book full of writing I can't read, and a hunk of metal that I don't understand the purpose of? There's so much to investigate that I don't know where to begin."

His snout lowered in a nod. "Your puzzles are bigger than most. But I think everyone feels overwhelmed when something unexplained enters their life. Like a Draksa, for instance." She laughed, and he continued, "But you're smart and you've chosen your partners well. I'm sure that between us, we'll find the answers you need."

She put her palms on the ground behind her, leaned back, closed her eyes, and rolled her neck. Being so busy had actually been good for her as it had removed any excuses she might have made to herself. There simply wasn't time to do anything that didn't make progress in some areas. "How about you and your answers?"

He snorted. "I chose my partners less well."

"Ha, ha. Don't avoid the question."

Fyre sounded less concerned than he'd been in previous discussions on the topic. "I still want to know why I can't remember things as well as I think I should. But it's not the most important thing in my life at the moment. We have so much to do and none of it requires me to recall everything."

She nodded, scrambled her feet, and stretched her back. "We have enough time left for a couple of rounds of one-on-one." She frowned and pointed. "No freezing. I won't be able to stand under a hot shower for twenty minutes to counteract it." His skill was sufficient to encase an opponent without doing real damage, but the last time he'd done it, she'd needed a whole day to return to feeling normal.

He laughed, sibilantly mocking her. They took up positions at opposite ends of the space and attacked simultaneously. She summoned her sticks as she ran and by the time they were in melee range, they were solidly in her grip. He bounded at her head and as always, she was surprised by how powerful his legs were. She slid beneath the attack, plowed a furrow in the dirt, and dragged the tip of one stick along his belly. The idea occurred to her that it might be possible to put points on them or even edges but for some reason, that struck her as different and more severe than using them as bludgeons.

She ran out of time to pursue that train of thought as the Draksa slithered in again. This particular movement was something he only did when attacking, and he resembled a snake in the way he shifted from side to side while he still advanced with amazing speed. She braced herself, and when he reared to bite at her arm, she brought a stick down on his snout. He'd assured her that even her strongest blow wouldn't damage him much unless she used magic and had demonstrated that his species healed quickly by deliberately cutting himself. In under a minute, the wound had disappeared as if it had never been. Still, she didn't plan to hit him in the skull if she could help it.

It redirected him but didn't stop the attack. He pushed off with his back legs and barreled into her. She tried to spin the instant she realized that was his plan but was only halfway through when he made contact. Cali fell and he landed on top of her immediately, his sharp teeth on her neck. She tapped out and he backed away. After taking a moment to wipe the dirt off her face, she bounced up. "Okay, scale brain. Let's see you do that again."

He laughed and trotted back to the starting position. She stared at him, then deliberately defocused to be ready for an attack from any direction. He didn't wait for a command but raced toward her. When he got close, she forced herself to relax. The Draksa went low this time and threw himself into a sideways roll at her feet. She caught a glimmer as she leapt over him and landed on the other side, twirled, charged, and yelled, "Cheater!" He'd told her about the magical armor his species could invoke at need. It wasn't long-lasting in most of them but could provide a distinct momentary advantage. She resisted blasting him with force and ran after him. He came out of the tumble facing her and leapt.

This time, she was ready and dipped to her right and twisted, bringing both sticks up to intercept his attack and guide him off course. She dove after him, and when he landed on his side, she flung herself on top of him. They wrestled and she attempted to get behind him and lock her arms and legs around his thick neck while he worked to twist and bring his claws into position to rake her.

They broke apart laughing after almost a minute of

struggling. She rolled onto her back, panting. "You had me. There was no way."

He lowered himself to the ground beside her, his face beside hers. "Probably. But it was a good move and if you were using magic instead of sticks, you could have ended it easily."

She nodded. "I may lack the killer instinct when it comes right down to it."

"I have enough for both of us."

"Really? But you seem so sweet." Her tone was an odd mixture of sincerity and sarcasm. He was sweet—to her and her friends—but she had little doubt he could turn vicious toward threats.

"Only until I need to not be."

Her leg hurt when she stood, and she realized she'd twisted her knee. "Damn. Hey, you can't do that healing thing on others, can you?"

His snout swung from side to side. "Nope. I seem to remember that magical healers exist, but I don't think they're Draksa."

Interesting. That's good to know. She sighed as a realization surfaced. *It probably means that jerk I fought in the abandoned building will be up and around much sooner than he has any right to be.* "Is your veil still up?"

"Of course."

"Excellent." She drew the magical circle in the air that connected here to there, in this case, the entry hallway in her new apartment. They stepped through and she removed her shoes and set them on the mat positioned there for that purpose. "Hey, lizard face. Get back here and wipe your feet. Paws. Whatever." He ignored her and tracked mud down the hallway. She looked at her phone and groaned, then called after him. "You're lucky I don't have time to deal with your complete lack of consideration right now. But you'll get yours."

The snort from deeper in the apartment showed exactly how concerned he was. She muttered, "Oh, you'll pay. You'll all pay. Just you wait."

CHAPTER TWENTY-TWO

After spending a large portion of the day in bed recovering from the encounter, Tanyith had dropped off the item he'd collected from Crain with Dray the night before. In return, he'd received a promise of further contact and a useful piece of information about the missing man. He didn't technically need to report to Sienna, but it was an opportunity to visit her again that he wasn't able to resist.

It hadn't taken her long to answer his text and agree to get together. She'd passed on his suggestion of coffee and invited him to her place, and he did his best not to read anything into that choice—or into the fact that she wanted to see him again. *It's totally about the missing dude. Positively. Well, almost surely. Probably.*

He halted the unproductive train of thought as he steered his bike to a stop in front of her house. *Maybe I lost my mind in prison and all this is merely a hallucination. That would explain everything really well.* He shook his head, removed his helmet, and raked a hand through his hair to push it into some semblance of a style. As he no longer knew the neighborhood, he carried the headwear with him to the porch. The door was opened before he arrived, and an eager-looking Sienna closed it after he entered.

Her excitement was palpable in the way she bounced as she walked and jumped onto the same couch she'd chosen last time. He took the expected seat across from her, and she poured him more of the same infused bourbon as before. Tanyith sipped it, satisfying her obligations as a host, then set it on the table before him. His face twisted in a smile tinged with the acknowledgment that her enthusiasm wasn't for him. "Hi, Sienna. How have you been?"

She laughed. "Fine. Don't be like that. Tell me."

Damn. I've always been about as impenetrable as a children's book to her. He shook his head. "It's nothing concrete. I texted you that."

The woman nodded, and her long blonde hair flopped into her face. She pushed it away in annoyance. "I know. I'm not expecting anything. But if you don't quit delaying, I'll start throwing things at you." She hurled a small pillow beside her by way of illustration, and he stilled his reflexes. It caught him in the face and made her laugh. "The next one will be much more painful."

He pulled his brain out of wherever it had gone wandering and chuckled. "All right, you've scared me into obedience. Please, oh please, no more wicked pillow tosses." He reached for the glass and took one more sip, and then was out of ways to delay the process. "Okay, so, while you knew him as Aiden Walsh, the people at the Stallion knew him as Adam Harlen. Does that name mean anything to you?"

She frowned but didn't reply and focused on her hands. He watched quietly, not sure if she was processing the information or searching through her memory. Finally, she shrugged and returned her gaze to his. "No. I've never heard it before. Whenever we were around other people, they called him Aiden, Walsh, or Harry. I never understood that last one, but maybe it has something to do with Harlan?"

Tanyith nodded. "It could have. I thought maybe you wouldn't know about the second name. It's not necessarily a bad sign. You know that many people in our...uh, line of work used aliases."

A little of the darkness that had swept over her left her expression and she nodded. "Right. That's right." She picked her glass up, tipped a fair amount past her lips, and poured a little more in. He waited while she swirled the ice and took a deep breath. "Okay, continue."

"Why do I feel like a bad student and you're the teacher?" He laughed.

She joined in with a chuckle. "Because you have a natural dislike of authority. Now, get back to saying useful things."

He steeled himself to deliver news that would probably hurt her. "My contact tells me he still visited the bar sometimes for a month or two after he vanished from your life."

She frowned, the expression filled with sadness. Her voice came out in a choked whisper. "What was he doing?" Seeing her so vulnerable made his stomach clench painfully.

"My contact didn't know. All he could say was that

Adam—well, Aiden—was definitely into something and seemed more stressed than usual about it."

Sienna uttered a dark laugh. "Since virtually nothing bothered him, that must have been a sight to see."

He nodded. "Then he vanished from there, too."

"And?"

Tanyith shrugged. "And that's where we're at right now. I have a few leads. He was seen with a couple of other people whom I didn't recognize from their descriptions, and D"—he coughed to cover the near revelation—"and this guy Raymond I talked to doesn't have their names. So it's another mystery to be solved."

Sienna sighed. "I'm not sure what I expected but this isn't it."

He offered her a soft smile. "I hear you. I assumed there'd be some difficulty following a lead this old but so far, everything I've discovered has been a surprise."

"It's good that you found someone who knew something, though. After all this time, I was afraid you might not be able to."

If only I could tell you how strangely that turned out. He'd made the decision not to reveal his source although he still wasn't sure if he was trying to protect See, trying to keep Dray to himself until he discovered what the hell was going on, or some other reason entirely. After he'd spun it around in his head, he'd decided to shove the issue in a locked box in his brain and continue to move forward. "Agreed. I thought that part would be harder. Apparently, you're lucky."

She laughed, but her response was lost in the sound of

loud simultaneous crashes from the front and the back of the house as all the windows in the room shattered.

Tanyith hurled himself reflexively across the space that separated him from Sienna, shoved her into the fortunately soft cushions, and covered her body with his own. He took several cuts to his head and neck before his force shield snapped into place to protect them. When the initial chaos faded, he stood quickly and pulled her to her feet. "Upstairs. Now."

She didn't argue and led the way to the house's second level. Sounds from below were consistent with multiple people entering from different directions. When the two of them reached the top, she led him into her bedroom. Memories flooded him, the space exactly as it had been when they'd been together, and he pushed them aside. She scrabbled under the bed and withdrew a knotted rope while he moved to the window facing the side of the house. He threw the latch and opened it in time for her to toss the weighted end out. The actions were as efficient as all the times they'd practiced it before he was sent away.

He stuck his head out to ensure no one waited below. This window had been chosen because it led to the narrow side of the yard, the one least likely to be used by enemies since there were no ground floor entrances or windows. He nodded and she climbed over and out while he returned to the doorway. When the first intruder appeared, he pounded the man with a force blast that hurled him down the stairs into his friends. The ubiquitous hoodie and long hair told him it was the Atlantean gang. Curses raced through most of his mind while the remainder counted the seconds it would take Sienna to reach the ground.

When the allotted time had passed, he slammed the door closed and shoved a dresser in front of it. He crossed to the window and used the rope to descend, knowing that every ounce of magical energy he had might be needed to fight the attackers. She was crouched near a hedge and stood when he reached the ground. "Where to?" she whispered

Tanyith admired the fact that she didn't waste time wondering who had broken in. Despite her free-spirited ways, she could be entirely practical when the situation called for it. He dug in his pocket and pressed his motor-cycle key into her hand. "Wait until I create a distraction in the back. Then, you go out the front. I'll watch in case but hopefully, it will draw them away. Head somewhere you haven't been since I came back—all the way out of the state if you need to. These are not people to mess with."

He'd expected an argument, but she simply nodded. *She's scared, and rightly so.* He pulled her into a hug and whispered, "You've got this. But move fast." He triggered a blast of force to launch himself up the three stories to the roof of her house. As he passed the window, he saw a face inside but didn't have time to damage it. He landed and stumbled but quickly found purchase on the inclined surface. There was a wooden swing set in the back yard, an inheritance from the previous owners of the house that Sienna had kept and used often. He shook his head at the imminent loss and reached for fire.

The ball of roiling flame struck the target cleanly and set it ablaze with a deafening whoosh. He didn't wait to see the reaction but turned and scuttled to the opposite side. Sienna's dark form raced into view on a direct trajectory toward the bike. A shadow detached from the blackness on the other side of the front yard and raced to intercept her. *Damn it. Competent enemies suck.* He flung himself off the roof and used a blast of force to drive the enemy to the ground and control his landing beside him.

Sienna's head whipped around and he yelled, "Go!"

The man at his feet tried to rise, and Tanyith kicked him in the ribs, then again in the skull. *There's no time for niceties.* The bike roared to life and the tires screeched as it accelerated down the street, and shouts came from the house in response. The smart move would have been to throw fire into the structure, but he couldn't bring himself to do it. *There's too much history. Plus, it would hurt her.* He growled with the guilt of having brought trouble to her doorstep. A shout indicated that another of the invaders had seen him and a second later, a blast of power rocketed into his chest and thrust him to the side.

He stumbled but managed to regain his footing and summoned his own magical attacks to launch hardened spheres of force about the size of billiard balls at his barely visible assailant. A cry of pain was lost almost instantly in the shouts of the others who raced around the corner and into view. Tanyith's eyes widened, and he turned and ran for his life.

CHAPTER TWENTY-THREE

The overhead lights were close enough to one another that he couldn't use the street or the sidewalk if he wanted to have any chance to escape the eyes of those in pursuit. He sprinted across the lane, ran into the yard of the house on the opposite side, and vaulted a low hedge like a hurdler seeking Olympic gold. *I bet they'd get a world record every time if there was someone trying to kill them.* He zigged and zagged as much as he could without sacrificing his lead, and the maneuver ensured that attacks from behind landed on either side of him.

I can't keep this up for long. Ahead was a house similar in size to Sienna's and when he was close enough, he blasted the ground with force magic to lift himself to the roof. A magical attack splashed off the wall near him, followed by a strike to the back that sent him tumbling. The pain arrived a moment later as the flames set his clothes afire, and he threw himself into a roll down the opposite side of the roof. He was in midair before he could stop himself, and while the force blast he cast beneath him saved him from major injury, he impacted with enough speed that he couldn't breathe for several precious seconds.

His failsafe plan was to portal out, but he didn't want to lead them to his home or to the basement of the tavern, which were his only options at the moment. His brain shouted at his body to move, and he rolled and came up again into a run. He caught a bright flash out of the corner of his eye and snapped his head around. A trident raced toward him. *A damned trident—what the hell?* He let himself fall to avoid it, which was easy since he had already tripped, and cursed as the trail of light it left behind curved toward where it had come from.

Obviously, his plan to flee was invalid in the face of an enemy with one of the trademark weapons of the Atlantean warriors. There was no possibility that he'd have time to portal and no chance of running fast or far enough to evade him. His mind shifted to finding the optimal way to engage him while not being overrun by the rest. Clearly, it was a no-rules attack since none of the formal niceties of challenge and acceptance had been observed. Essentially, that meant he was free to do what he really wanted to do anyway. He raced down a natural funnel created by two driveways side by side, stopped, and spun.

While he waited for the enemy to appear, his gaze roamed in all directions to guard against the sudden appearance of the trident, but he was reasonably sure he'd put the houses between himself and the warrior. When the first attackers appeared in a concerted charge, he smiled. If they'd stopped to attack, his plan would have been much less effective. He had counted on them wanting to make it personal. When the space was full and his foes had almost reached him, he swept his arms wide and delivered a horizontal sheet of fire into the Atlanteans. They screamed, fell, and began to roll to extinguish the flames. He bulldozed through them, kicking those who tried to stop him, and repeated the attack on a few who hadn't entered the funnel in time.

He'd bought himself a couple of minutes, which would hopefully be enough to lead the enemy leader away from his minions. *Of course, if he wants to let me escape, that would be fine too.* Tanyith laughed as his feet pounded the ground. *My luck's not that good.*

As expected, his pursuer hadn't given up during the weaving chase he had led him on. The man had only tried to throw the trident once more, and after the very near miss, he'd become smarter about avoiding straight routes. He'd done all he could to lose him—going over some buildings, through others, and around many more—but the Atlantean warrior refused to be shaken off. When the gang had spoken of the elite fighters of their homeland, it had always been with a mixture of reverence and fear. No one wanted to find themselves at the pointy end of the giant fork.

The location he had aimed for was directly ahead. An old middle school, damaged by floodwaters and since abandoned, stood alone in a large rectangle of grass and pavement. In his day, it had been a place to stage operations from and stash hot items in. He'd investigated it shortly after his return to the city and found it deserted.

One of his caches had been buried nearby and fortunately, had been undisturbed when he retrieved it.

The doors were blocked with a chain and padlock. Once upon a time, he'd had a key, but that was in the distant past. He threw a two-handed blast of force at them, ripped them from their rusted hinges, and hurled the metal rectangles into the building. They clanged as he pounded over them and past lockers on the right-hand side and the office area on the left. He turned barely in time to avoid the trident that would have caught him in the back if he'd gone straight and growled a curse. At the next turn, he darted into a hallway that ran parallel to the first. His objective was at the back corner and he arrived there a full ten seconds before his pursuer, which allowed him to catch a few breaths.

The Atlantean warrior sauntered into the cafeteria as if he hadn't a care in the world. *He probably thinks he doesn't. Of course, he might be right.* Tanyith shook his head. This situation was not something he'd ever even considered a possibility. His foe wore what seemed to be military trousers and boots, plus a black t-shirt. His muscles rippled under the apparel, and he walked like he knew the image he projected. Again, he probably did, given that he'd doubtless fought for position since childhood. His voice was deep and dismissive. "You should lie down. It would save us both trouble and lessen your pain."

From his position across the room with rows of tables separating them, Tanyith shook his head. "And you could simply leave."

The man shrugged. "I have my duty to perform." Glowing translucent armor wrapped around his wrists, hands, and shins in the same shade as the electric blue of his trident. Tanyith concentrated and summoned force versions of his sai. He much preferred the actual metal daggers to the magical ones, as these required him to concentrate to maintain their solidity and a distraction at the wrong moment could easily get him killed.

His opponent made a sharp gesture, and the tables collided noisily as they tumbled toward him. He threw a wall of force in their path while he segmented the part of his mind that maintained the sai and ran to his left in case the barrier failed. The warrior gave a satisfied smile and rushed to intercept him. The trident lashed out, and he caught it on the curved guard of his lead sai, rotated the weapon to lock it against his opponent's, and yanked it to the side. He stepped forward and stabbed with the other one, but a quick downward block of the magical bracer on the man's forearm stopped it cold. His foe snapped that fist out at his face, and he disengaged and jumped aside to avoid the sweep of the freed trident.

The Atlantean laughed. "You are not worthy of this battle. A child could defeat you."

Tanyith shook his head. "Whatever. If you were so confident, you wouldn't have brought your little army along."

The blonde-bearded man scowled. "That was not my choice."

He shrugged. "Nevertheless, whoever told you to do it clearly didn't think you were up to the task. Why is that, I wonder? Could it be that a girl half your size kicked your friend's ass? I bet that's it."

His opponent didn't reply but used his weapon to

conjure three force beams that he swept across at chest height to try to slice him in half. Tanyith dropped and rolled to get under the attack and threw a fireball as he bounced to his feet. It struck his foe in the stomach but failed to ignite his clothes. For a moment, he was wreathed in flame before the attack vanished. *Damn it.*

The hasty plan hadn't included anything other than evening the odds. He didn't know anyone who had ever fought an Atlantean warrior, much less defeated one. *Except Cali, and she didn't explain how she did it.* He shook his head. *If I die at the hands of this dude, she'll find a way to resurrect me so she can taunt me about failing where she succeeded. I'd better find a way to survive.*

As motivations went, it was worse than most but better than some. The problem was that he didn't know how to hurt the man. His mind sifted through options but discarded them as fast as they appeared. *Blow him up with gas. No, the utilities are shut off. Electrocute him, but I have the same problem. Stab him.* He dodged to the side as the trident poked at his face. *Okay, no, his weapon is too long for that.* Tanyith jumped into the gap that had been created behind the tables when they'd impacted the wall and sent his own blast of force forward to propel them toward the other man. He turned and leapt through the windows behind him, using a curved slab of force to protect him as he did so.

When he landed, he turned to watch the snarling man bat away the last of the tables. He smiled and shattered all the windows with a loud clap and hurled the broken shards at his foe. The warrior spun his trident in a blurred circle and intercepted the incoming projectiles. But they were only meant as a distraction since his first plan to beat him in a mostly fair one-on-one had failed.

A key feature of the school that had led them to use it as a hideout had been a nearby underground bunker, probably a relic of the Cold War. It had been damp and generally gross, but they'd set it up as a final position for defense against an attacking force. He shook his head as he ran to where he remembered the entrance to be. *We always imagined we'd face the police or something. It never entered the realm of possibility we'd have to defend ourselves against one of our own.*

The warrior roared in anger behind him, and Tanyith dove and rolled to avoid a potential attack. A blast of force rippled the air over his head. *Too close.* He found the heavy metal disc and yanked on it, to no avail. A look at his opponent showed him climbing out through the window. *He's like the damn terminator or something.* Out of time, he blasted the cover free and leapt in after it. The seven-foot drop was easy and the dark hallway was ominous. He conjured a light in one hand and raced ahead, carefully avoiding the tripwires they'd so cleverly placed long before. Lack of use had allowed the water to seep in and the smell of mold and decay was almost overwhelming. *Come on. Follow me in, you big jerk.* A thump signaled that he'd received his wish, and he turned the corner at the far end.

The ladder was rusty but the trapdoor overhead was still intact. He backed away from the area and blasted an angled force burst that removed the wooden barrier. From behind him came a popping sound and a shout of anger. *That'll be the pepper spray. It's great that it still worked.* The traps were mainly physical, except for the final one he'd magically armed as he raced past. They also increased in effectiveness as one progressed. He stood under the open hole in the ceiling and looked at the maintenance building for the school, then lowered his gaze to await the appearance of his enemy.

The warrior rounded the corner, his face a mask of rage and murder, and Tanyith offered him a cheery wave and used a force blast to hurl himself up and through the opening. His foe's growl was lost in the sound of explosions and a rush of water that filled and then collapsed the tunnel. It had been their last resort defense and the only fatal one, which was why it had required magic to shatter the first layer of plastic panels that held it in place behind the walls. The tripwire activated two hand grenades that broke the last barrier, which was only glass. It was lucky that the explosives still worked and the second layer of resistance was still whole.

He didn't think the warrior could survive it, but he had seen too many movies to count on it. When he broke out of the building, he ran and as soon as he felt he'd reached a reasonable distance and portaled to the only place where he knew he'd be safe. The basement of the Drunken Dragons tavern was dark and chilly, but perfect. He drank half the healing potion he carried in a metal container in his pocket, conjured a sphere of warmth around himself, and succumbed to sleep. His second-to-last thought before unconsciousness claimed him was to hope that Sienna had made it to safety. The last one was a mental groan at the realization that he would need to buy another motorcycle.

CHAPTER TWENTY-FOUR

After several sessions during the week since she'd begun training in mental magic with Emalia, Cali began to feel that she had made significant progress. Her mentor had taught her different approaches and different metaphors but overall, it came down to the same things—piercing the defenses, priming the target for a distraction, and delivering the distraction. She'd managed to increase her speed and her confidence, and today's efforts had been the best so far. They'd practiced upstairs, but Emalia had insisted on a break before they continued and of course, that meant tea and cookies in the downstairs kitchenette area.

Cali took a sip from her cup of tea and lowered it to the table. "So, what's next?"

Her teacher nibbled at the edge of a rectangle of shortbread before she set it daintily on the china plate in front of her. "Your skills are reliable in what we've practiced so far, so we are free to move on to new things. My thought is more direct influences."

"Like mind control?" She was still more than a little freaked out over the idea that it was possible to use another being as a puppet.

Emalia sighed. "No. Simply causing an action rather than a reaction."

"More explaining and less being mysterious, please."

The older woman laughed. "Consider it like provoking a reflex. While you can't make someone do a large chain of activities or something complicated, you could do smaller things."

She thought about it. "Like making them sneeze at the wrong moment?"

Her aunt stretched across the table and tapped her on the forehead with her index finger. "Now you're getting it." She leaned back. "That would be at the easiest end of the range. Harder would be making them drop something they were holding since they'd have a competing desire to hang onto it. But things like that are certainly possible."

Cali yawned and stretched. "I think maybe that's a little much for today, though."

"I have something else for us, anyway."

"What?"

Her teacher grinned. "I visited the library and learned a little about the charm your parents left you."

She leaned forward and put her elbows on the table so quickly that the cups rattled in their saucers. "Oh, tell me more."

"It's a shield charm, as we thought. There are several possible activation words, but I couldn't find any clear indication that one would be better than another or if these are all the possibilities. We'll have to use trial and error to determine which one."

Cali shrugged. "It seems simple enough."

Emalia exhaled a small sigh. "With magic, everything has a risk. The improper word could have unintended consequences."

She frowned. "Why?"

The older woman raised a hand as if beseeching the universe for understanding. "Magicals are not immune to paranoia or self-delusion. Sometimes, there are traps to prevent theft or misuse."

"But my parents wouldn't have done that."

"And if we were positive that this was created by them, we could be confident that it was safe. But all we know is that they had it and that they wanted you to have it."

"I trust them. And if anything does go wrong, you're right here. So let's give it a try."

Emalia looked hesitant but nodded. She extended the charm, and Cali clipped it awkwardly onto the necklace she wore. Her mentor had performed a series of detection spells that she claimed proved it was nothing dangerous, and she had immediately started wearing it as a way to feel closer to her parents.

"Okay, what's the first one?"

"*Clypeus*. And it's not enough to simply say it. You must also will the shield into being."

She rolled her eyes. "There's always fine print with you. What?"

Her aunt laughed. "When you say the word, you have to also actively want to be shielded from harm. Put that in the front of your mind."

She suppressed several potential smartass remarks and nodded. "Okay." She brought the idea of a protective barrier that looked much like one of Fyre's ice attacks to her mind and whispered, "*Clypeus.*" She waited expectantly, but nothing happened.

"Apparently, it's not that one, then. Try *Clypeum.*"

They worked through all the versions of several different words without any effect until they reached the last third of the list. When Cali whispered "*Aspida,*" a glimmer appeared in the air around her but faded quickly.

Emalia leaned forward. "That's the one, then, but you need to concentrate harder to activate it." She held a hand up to stop the girl from doing so. "Since there were no other matching charms in the bag your parents left, I've worked under the assumption that it's reusable, but it's also possible that it will be consumed if you cast it. Now that we've stumbled on the word without invoking the spell, do you want to try it now or wait for an emergency?"

As always, Cali wanted to know but restrained herself with a frown. "It seems stupid to use it without a reason if it's a one-shot. Let's wait."

The woman nodded and looked uncomfortable. "When I was at the library, I found something out about the sword that seems to connect with the Atlanteans' attack on you."

She perked up. The lack of understanding had gnawed at her, and she hadn't had a single idea about how to resolve it other than relying on Emalia to find something out or asking Zeb to inquire among his friends. She'd held off on the latter to see if her teacher could make any headway. "What did you find?"

"We have to start with a brief history lesson." Emalia stood to refill both teacups, set the pot down, and remained standing. "In ancient Atlantis, there were two routes to power. First, you could be born into the right family."

"Royalty?" Cali interrupted.

Emalia waggled a hand. "Kind of, but not exactly like you know the term. More like a council formed of several ruling families, a member of which would hold the position of monarch at any given time. But the remainder still wielded significant influence."

She nodded doubtfully. "Okay, gotcha. And the second way?"

"Ritual combat."

"So anyone could essentially become royal?"

Her aunt snorted. "Of course not. The trials were to determine who could compete to be monarch. They did allow one commoner each time a Rite of Succession was invoked, but they didn't usually last very long. In any case, one version of the rite that I found described included battles with a delay between them. The gang might be using a ritual approach to attacking you. When the woman said, 'next level,' it probably meant something like next round."

Cali frowned. "Why on Earth or Oriceran would they do that?"

Her teacher sat again and looked her in the eye. "I can't be certain, but that might have something to do with the blade piece your parents left you. I found a picture of a sword with similar markings, and the story that ran alongside it told of an artifact weapon that had been broken in battle and the pieces gathered and distributed among the royal families at the time."

The implication hit her, and she whispered, "Holy Hell."

Emalia nodded. "Exactly. It's extremely likely that at some point in your history, your family was royalty. And it's completely guaranteed that you'll be attacked again when the week they promised is up."

"Maybe we should have Karaoke on Wednesdays." Zeb's voice was teasing but Cali wasn't in the most receptive of moods since half her brain still tried to process the revelations from earlier in the day.

"Maybe you should simply accept that some nights are slower than others." The customers had been steady and surprisingly needy, but the extra attention she'd provided hadn't resulted in increased tips, a situation she found highly annoying.

Her irritation only made his grin grow wider. He spoke as if he were thinking deeply. Internally, she called it his "philosopher's voice." Externally, she accused him of being slow-minded most of the times he used it. "A second game night each month, maybe."

She rolled her eyes. "Heaven forbid. One is more than enough. I'd prefer the Karaoke."

The front door opened and Tanyith walked in, a shiny black motorcycle helmet under his arm. He handed it over, and Zeb stashed it behind the bar. She asked, "So?"

He nodded. "Yeah. They had eyes on the place." He'd

been out to check on his apartment. "I found watchers guarding virtually every way in."

"Will you portal?"

"No. It's far too likely that there will be a trap waiting for me. There's nothing of real value left behind. Most importantly, Sienna texted and she's safe."

Zeb clapped briskly. "That's worthy of a toast." He pulled three short glasses of cider and handed them out. "To Sienna."

They replied in kind, clinked glasses, and drank. "So, should we skip meeting the ship, then?" she asked.

Tanyith shook his head decisively. "Absolutely not. The faster we dig to the bottom of all this garbage, the faster we'll be able to get out from under it and return to our normal lives."

"There's nothing normal about you, dude," she quipped,

Zeb replied, "I'm the only normal one among us."

She laughed. "Oh yeah, totally." She turned to Tanyith. "So, what are you hoping to get out of the boat people?" Someone shouted her name from behind her, and she held a hand up with a sigh. "Wait a sec." She twisted and yelled, "What?" before she headed toward the complaining patron. One thing led to another, and she returned to the conversation after a twenty-minute delay and clambered onto her high seat again. "Okay, where were we?"

The dwarf laughed. "Discussing why Fyre is so much smarter than you." A snort from the floor behind the bar registered the Draksa's support for the comment.

Cali called, "Shut up, you," but it was filled with affection. She pointed Zeb. "And you, buddy, if you know what's good for you."

She faced Tanyith with a fake smile. "You were saying?"

"I guess there's a lot on the table here. First, we want to see if the Atlantean gang actually is meeting them at the docks and whether they're using offers or threats to get them to come here. I really hope it's the former. That's how we would have done it in my time. And the fact that the new arrivals are socialized in the islands before coming here makes that seem more likely."

"Are we okay with it, if it is?"

He shrugged. "Not entirely, at least for me, but I don't know any better way to help the newcomers at this point. We can work that angle once we have more information."

The response was disappointing, not because he didn't have a plan but because she hated the idea of new arrivals being immediately pulled into the gang's influence. Unfortunately, she lacked any other ideas at the moment. "Okay. What if it's threats?"

Tanyith gave a crooked smile. "Well, that's easier. We stop it."

"And then what happens to the people?"

"I guess we'll need to loop Barton in—or a more appropriate police division."

Cali laughed. "She'll be around there anyway, I'm sure."

He nodded. "Yeah. She wouldn't give us the info and not arrive to see what we do with it."

"Do you miss her?"

With a sigh, he turned to Zeb. "Refill?" He extended his glass and the dwarf took it. After fortifying himself with a few slow sips, Tanyith answered her question. "Not nearly as much as I miss the serenity of life before I knew you."

She stuck her tongue out at him. "So you'd rather go

back to prison? We could probably make that happen for you."

He shook his head. "Don't even joke about that."

"You're right. That was unfair. I'm sorry." She paused for a moment, then asked, "So, is that everything?"

"No. There are a couple of other things we need to find out. First, are the Zatoras kidnapping and imprisoning people from the ships? If so, we determine how that's happening and make it stop." She nodded in complete agreement. "Second, are there any other Atlantean gang activities going on with the ships? It seems logical that they'd choose portals wherever they can, but maybe not. Logically, if you have access to a giant boat, it makes sense that you'd use it."

He shrugged. "Finally, I guess if both groups are working the docks, how do they manage not to fight over it? Do they have some kind of agreement? If so, we could possibly mess that up for them sometime in the future."

She sighed. "It'll feel like an eternity between now and then."

"Fill the time with work," Zeb suggested. He pointed to the room at her back.

"Yeah, yeah. Whatever."

Once the tavern's last customer had staggered out the door and it was locked behind him, she rejoined the men who had chatted on and off throughout the evening. "Have you come up with anything new?"

Zeb shook his head. "We've discussed his investigation."

She hopped onto the chair, grateful to finally be off her feet. "What's up?"

Tanyith shrugged. "More questions than answers. I discovered an old friend of mine posing as a human, apparently as part of an anti-magical gang. He told me I should join but he seems to be under surveillance so we haven't been able to talk freely. I'm not even sure he's still anything like the guy I knew." He sounded sad about it. "Anyway, the person I'm trying to find appears to have vanished about six months ago. I gathered the names of people he was seen hanging around with so now, I need to find them."

Cali shook her head. "It seems like a ton of work to go through to make a buck. Hey, maybe you could do Zeb's job. You certainly couldn't be more annoying than he is."

They both chuckled. Tanyith replied, "It's not about the money. I have enough to last a little while longer. It's about finding him for Sienna."

"So." She leaned in as if to be conspiratorial and whispered, "Is she your girl, then? Your main dame? Your femme fatale?"

He rolled his eyes and Zeb made a sour face. The dwarf replied, "Ageism. That's what it is. A complete lack of respect for her elders."

She turned and pointed. "Aha. You admit you're elderly. Fyre, take note of this moment. We have a senior citizen among us." The Draksa snorted but didn't otherwise move from his curled position near the stew pot. Zeb threw a bar cloth and it smacked her in the face. She pulled it away and frowned. "That was uncalled for."

He shook his head. "Completely called for. You're a menace."

She grinned. "And proud of it."

Tanyith stood and stretched. "It's time to head to one of the hotels in the quarter. I've already let the landlord know I won't come back to the old run-down place. I'll find another apartment once this mess is over. Text me if you need me."

Cali felt sorry for him, and the words were out of her mouth before she realized what she was doing. "You could stay with me—with Fyre and I. Um, we have a couch. The last tenants left it. You could use it."

To his credit, he didn't make anything of it, which meant she didn't need to retract the offer or punch him in the face. He asked, "Are you sure?"

She nodded. "Yep. We're partners. It's our job to look out for each other, right?"

"That's certainly a big part of my definition of the word," Zeb interjected. He looked at the dragon lizard at his feet. "What do you think, my sleepy friend?"

Fyre raised his head and moved it up and down in a nod.

Cali gestured toward him. "There you go. The freeloader has spoken and wishes to add another freeloader to the tally for a couple of nights." She grinned to make sure he knew she was teasing. "Let's do this." She created a portal to connect the tavern to her apartment and stepped through. Fyre followed a moment later and Tanyith was a few steps behind him.

Zeb called, "Goodnight, folks. Be safe tomorrow."

She yelled, "Maybe you and Valerie should join us."

He shook his head without a word and waved his arm to collapse her portal and prevent her from adding any of the teasing comments she had on hand. She pointed at the couch. "Yours." She pointed at the door to the bedroom. "Mine." Then, she gestured to include the whole apartment. "Fyre's." They laughed together and she opened the door to her bedroom. "Seriously, make yourself at home. I have the dojo in the morning, so Fyre and I will leave way too early. You're welcome to whatever things might be edible in the fridge or the cupboards."

He nodded. "Thanks, Cali. I really appreciate it."

She smiled and closed the door. *Get us all through tomorrow night without injury and you'll have more than repaid the favor.*

CHAPTER TWENTY-FIVE

Cali was surprised to find Tanyith waiting outside with Fyre when her Aikido class ended. He was dressed in jeans and a t-shirt and sat beside the Draksa, his eyes closed against the midday sun. She thought he looked healthier than he had when they'd first met and the tension he always seemed to carry in his posture appeared to be less intense than usual. Which, given that they would potentially be in the presence of the two gangs that had legitimate reasons to want to cause them pain, was unexpected.

He tilted his head up when she blocked the sunlight. "Hey. Was it a good class?"

She shrugged. "Fairly good. Sensei said my mind wasn't in it. Apparently, there's something big happening today that's a distraction."

"That's why I'm here." He nodded. "I woke up seven times last night and each time, it was like my brain tried to tell me that I had missed something important. I really don't have any idea what it is so I've called in some outside help. I thought you'd want to come along."

"We're going to Emalia's for a reading? I bet she'd love to get some insight into the mess that is your life."

He laughed. "I wouldn't throw stones, there, Cali. Have you solved any of the mysteries your parents left behind for you?"

She placed a hand on her heart. "Ouch. You wound me." She frowned. "I'm sweaty and wearing an old t-shirt and ugly shorts. You gave me enough time to get it together, right?"

"As long as you do it fast. We have forty-five minutes, and we'll have to take a car to the garden district."

"Okay. I can work with that."

Twenty-five minutes later, the car pulled away from the Drunken Dragons, where they'd portaled to meet it. Cali had done her best to keep her relocation to Dasante's building hidden from anyone who might be watching her. The easiest way to accomplish that was to use the Tavern as a transit point, given that she had the key and Zeb was usually there anyway.

When Tanyith had mentioned that they would meet a Drow Elf, Fyre had perked up and insisted he come with them. She'd been unwilling to argue and since being ambushed, she preferred having him with her on most occasions. He was a black Rottweiler today, and although the driver had looked askance at him, his presence hadn't proved to be a problem.

They exited the car and tied Fyre's leash to a parking meter. The inside of The Bulldog was shady and comfort-able, and the bar ran a long way back from where it began near the door. Behind it, fifty draft taps, each with its own cleverly designed handle, added character. It was fairly empty, being after lunch and before happy hour, and the woman seated on one of the high stools did nothing to hide her lineage and was thus easily recognizable. She had ebony skin, white hair, and long, thin limbs. Her dress left much of her flesh bare while simultaneously didn't appear to be very revealing at all. *That's a clever trick. Maybe I can get her to explain how she does it.*

Cali scrounged a bowl of water from the bartender and took it outside to Fyre. She knelt beside him and whispered, "Is there anything you know about Drow that I should be aware of?" The only member of the race she'd had contact with was Zeb's friend, and then only in passing.

"They are smart." he whispered in response, "and about as prone to violence as Atlanteans." *Which is saying something.* "Also, they're often very powerful with magic. Not many have come to Earth as far as I know. Of course, my memory isn't the best." He chuckled, which was a positive sign. A few days before, he wouldn't have been able to laugh about it.

She ran a hand down his back. His scales were fully metallic now and shone brilliantly in the sun. "Thanks."

"Be careful."

"Stay out of trouble." He barked at her, and she laughed and escaped from the heat into the building. As she approached, Tanyith and the woman stood and he gestured them both to a table. Glasses of cider appeared for all of them moments later when the bartender swept past.

Her partner said, "Caliste Leblanc, this is Nylotte. She's the one who got me out of the prison."

Her eyes widened. "Wow. I guess you owe her, huh."

The Dark Elf waved that idea away. "I had an obligation to a third party. Tanyith is merely the lucky beneficiary of a number of random chances."

Cali nodded. "Damn lucky, I'd say, given what I've heard about the place."

Tanyith shivered. "Every word is true. And, hey, how about we not talk about it anymore? Nylotte, were you able to dig anything up?"

"Yes. And the information you gave me about the sword piece you found is of roughly the same value, so our accounts are even again. The cruise ship is operated by a series of shell companies that effectively disguise its ownership. What's interesting is that it isn't a publicly held company, which means all the capital to build it had to come from somewhere other than stock issues."

Cali frowned. "A loan?"

She shrugged. "One hell of a big loan, if so."

"So you think there's some funny business in there," Tanyith said.

Nylotte sighed. "Let's engage in a flight of fancy for a moment. Let's say that you have built a city in the epicenter of the location where ships and planes and people mysteriously go missing so often that a whole superstition has been built up around it. What's more likely —that it's the place doing it or that it's the people who secretly live there?"

Cali tilted her head, intrigued. "You're talking about the Bermuda Triangle."

The woman's sarcasm was as sharp as a needle. "You're right, Tanyith, she is smart and has a complete and total grasp of the obvious. Well done. Should we order you a cookie?" Something about the way she said it allowed her to take the comment as a joke rather than an insult, and she laughed.

"Chocolate chip, please. And if I can have two, also oatmeal."

The Dark Elf bared her teeth in a grin. "I think I like this one. Anyway, yes, the triangle. And if they've brought ships and planes down, or if they're merely salvaging what they find at the bottom of the ocean, they could build a fairly good down-payment given enough time."

Tanyith frowned. "So you're suggesting that even when Atlantis existed, they were already working on New Atlantis?"

She shrugged. "Is it so hard to believe, really? People with power always devise grandiose plans their constituents don't know about. It's apparently in the job description."

"So, the entire ship is suspect?" Cali asked. "That's what you're saying, basically. That it's a big floating potential enemy."

The Drow nodded. "That's exactly what I'm saying. There's no telling what's going on with it."

The man at the table suddenly startled like he'd been pricked with a pin. "Is it safe to let it in here? Couldn't it be carrying some kind of device? What if they wanted to wipe out the city or something?"

Nylotte nodded. "Good thinking. I'm already on that angle. If it's allowed to arrive, it will be because it's free of any weapon that could do significant damage. Of course, it is a ship filled with considerable fuel and such, so it could never be considered completely safe."

"Who would stop it?" Cali frowned. "Like, the Coast Guard or something?"

The other woman grinned. "Or something. Friends of mine. They work for the government."

"Do you work for the government?"

Her laugh was a joyful, chiming thing. "Gods of Earth and Oriceran, no. You're too funny."

Her face must have displayed her confusion because Tanyith laughed. "She doesn't exactly operate entirely on the legal side of the line. She...uh, what was the phrase... sells things of questionable providence."

"Ah, like Invel."

The Drow scoffed. "Invel. Please. He's a dabbler—a smart male but talks too much and is not at my level."

Okay, apparently, we have professional pride in our work. "Sorry, I didn't mean to offend."

The elf waved casually again. "Anyway, if the ship docks, you don't have to worry about it doing anything worse than blowing up. And I'll be nearby, just in case, to help out."

Tanyith's head snapped around to face her. "You will?"

She nodded. "I'm curious about this. The gang situation is one thing, but that feels localized to New Orleans. Not that it's any less important because of it. But there's been a fair amount of noise about Atlantis and Atlanteans lately, and maybe this is part of that. It's worth hanging around, having a nice dinner, and lurking on the docks for an evening."

Cali frowned. "I hate to say this, but if we really think this might be something bigger than it seems, we should give Barton a heads-up."

Nylotte's expression turned questioning, and Tanyith explained, "Detective Kendra Barton. New Orleans Police, anti-gang division."

She nodded. "And Tanyith's girlfriend."

He sighed and put his head on the table. "She. Is. Not. My. Girlfriend." His voice was muffled but still effectively displayed his exasperation. The two women laughed together.

The Drow raised an eyebrow and regarded her curiously. "I like you more and more. So, is his lover a good detective?"

Tanyith sputtered a denial, which made them both laugh again. Cali answered, "Well, I'm not sure they ever manage to have any actual conversation."

He shook his head. "Enough. Yes, she's a good detective. No, we're not dating nor lovers. Yes, we should let her know to keep her eyes open." He looked at Nylotte. "Honestly, you're as bad as she is. Shouldn't you be more mature?"

She scowled. "Were you going to reference my age?"

His eyes widened and he paled. "No, of course not."

The Drow winked at Cali. "Excellent. So, we're agreed. You'll alert the woman you are embarrassed to talk about but who isn't your girlfriend nor your lover about the potential for trouble at the docks. I'll be watching, so try not to make idiots of yourselves tonight."

Tanyith asked, "And the other thing?"

She nodded. "As agreed, the bag will be delivered to the

Drunken Dragons Tavern at five o'clock. Since the ship isn't due in until nine, that should give you sufficient time to get ready."

He stood. "We'd best get to it. Thank you again."

"You're welcome. And thank you for the information you provided in exchange." She gave Cali a smile. "Be safe, Cali. You remind me of a friend of mine and she constantly winds up taking on challenges that might get her killed. Try to be smarter."

I'm happy not to choose those kinds of challenges but someone needs to make them stop choosing me. "I'll do my best."

She smiled wider. "I'm sure that will be adequate." The Drow stood and sauntered out of the bar without a good-bye. They watched her go and turned to face each other.

He laughed. "You suck, you know that?"

"And you're way too easy. So, she's good people?"

"She is. I have trusted her with my life and I would again."

"Then you're glad she's watching the docks tonight?"

"Except for the part where if we make a mistake, she'll never let us forget it." He grinned.

Cali laughed. "It seems like you have a habit of attracting willful women who enjoy mocking you, Tanyith."

He seemed ready argue, then shook his head. "Shut up. Let's go get Fyre and prep for later."

When they stepped outside, they found the Drow leaning against the building and staring at Fyre. Cali asked, "Is there a problem?"

"That is not a dog," she replied,

"No, he isn't. Fyre, this is Nylotte. Nylotte, Fyre."

The Dark Elf turned to face her. "He's a Draksa, but not like any I've seen before."

Cali gave her a sharp look. "You've seen others?"

She nodded absently. "Yes. And there's something off about this one."

"My mentor told me he's much smarter than average."

Nylotte tapped a finger against her chin. "Is he? Hmm. Well, perhaps that's it." She shrugged and assumed a neutral expression before she turned and walked down the street.

Cali frowned. "What the hell was that about?" No one provided an answer.

CHAPTER TWENTY-SIX

The basement of the Drunken Dragons Tavern was once again strewn with gear for an upcoming operation. Janice was upstairs tending to the customers while Zeb oversaw their preparations. Fyre had made it abundantly clear that he wouldn't be left behind, so that was one issue addressed. He'd again agreed to stay hidden by a veil if events permitted him to do so.

They donned the same equipment belts as before, Tanyith's holding his sai and his healing and energy potions and hers carrying the same flasks and her Escrima sticks. They'd stopped at Emalia's long enough to learn the command for the shield charm, and she murmured *aspida* over and over in her mind. Her teacher had assured her that thinking it or even saying it without supplying magic and intentionality wouldn't trigger the spell. Still, she was nervous about letting the word cross her lips.

Nylotte had provided them each with a leather jacket that fit like a second skin. How the Drow had judged their sizes—especially hers since they'd never met before that day—was a mystery. But she'd promised Tanyith that the bespelled garb would protect them better than normal leather from bullets and blades. It was all she'd been able to do on short notice, apparently, but Cali was already a huge fan of her coat. "I look great in this. Seriously. It's perfect."

Zeb laughed. "It's good to see you caring about your appearance for a change."

Without turning away from the small mirror she used, Cali extended a single finger at him and drew a heartier laugh.

Tanyith said, "Do we need to go over the plan one last time?"

Fyre snorted, and she sighed. "No. We've all got it. We go. We watch. If we see the gangs only chatting to people off the ship, we leave it alone and keep watching. If they cause trouble, we go in and cause more trouble for them. If we see both gangs…well, we improvise."

He nodded. "And if something big happens?"

"Run like hell and let the Drow and Barton handle it. What did she say, by the way? Or did you spend the whole time being lovey-dovey?" He had excused himself from the Tavern to make the call, which allowed her and Zeb to laugh at him behind his back.

With a growl, he said, "We are not interested in each other. Get it through that thick slab of bone that stands in for your brain. She appreciated the heads-up and will take, quote, adequate precautions."

So many jokes leapt to her mind, but she decided to spare her partner, who seemed to be fragile over the issue. She changed the subject loudly. "So, Zeb, you'll be able to handle the bar and keep an ear out for our arrival?"

He nodded and pointed at two walls. "I've installed motion sensors. If you portal in, I'll get a flashing light upstairs so I can come and make sure you're not dead."

"Excellent." She snapped her fingers. "Tanyith, I had an idea. You should ask Nylotte if she has healing and energy potions that will work on Draksa, just in case." She thought about it for a second, then corrected herself. "Healing only. Fyre on an energy potion wouldn't be good for anyone, really." The Draksa snorted at her from his position atop a stack of crates, but Zeb's presence kept his sharp tongue quiet. She wasn't quite sure why he'd chosen to speak in front of Tanyith but not her boss, but that was a mere drop in the bucket of the things she didn't understand about her companion.

"I can do that." He pulled more unfamiliar items out of the satchel that had been delivered a half-hour earlier, as the Drow had promised, and which had provided their jackets. The next to emerge were three straps with a small box on them. He handed two to her. "Locators of some kind. She told us we needed to wear them."

Cali frowned. "Are they magical?"

He shrugged. "Who knows? Magical, half-and-half, all technology—it could be any of them."

"Why does she need us to have them?"

He strapped his over the arm of his coat. "I don't know, but if she says we should do it, I'll do it." She mirrored his actions.

Zeb chuckled. "That is always a good attitude when working with that one." He took the longer strap from Cali and moved toward Fyre.

She asked, "You know Nylotte?"

The dwarf put the locator around the Draksa's neck, pulled the Velcro apart, and reset it twice before he was satisfied. "I know of her. She ticks Invel off. He thinks she's too much of a 'free spirit.'" He made finger quotes in the air. "Of course, he probably thinks anyone born after him suffers from the same malady."

They laughed together at that, and Tanyith withdrew the final items from the bag and tossed it aside. Two hard cases contained what looked like sunglasses. She accepted hers from him and put them on, and the slightly dark cellar was suddenly as visible as being outdoors at high noon. She peered into all the places where shadows had held sway. "Oooh. Night vision, kind of." He waved his hand in front of his eyes.

"But without all the icky green ghostly stuff you see in video games. Nice." He took his off and put them carefully into their protective carrier, then slipped it into a pocket. With a heavy exhale, he checked the straps of the backpack he'd donned and said, "I think we're ready."

She nodded. "Me too. Fyre?" His snout dipped in agreement. "Okay, Zeb, let's make it happen."

The dwarf rotated one hand in a circle and a rift appeared in the air. On the opposite side, Vizidus, the wizard who had brokered the meeting with the two gangs in the tavern, waved at them to come over with a cross look on his face. They complied, and the passage closed the instant they were through.

Their escort was surprisingly spry, given his aged appearance. Cali considered asking him if he used magic for energy and if he could teach her to be faster or stronger, but decided it wasn't the time. *Next time he's in the*

Dragons, though, we'll have a chat. He led them along a series of side streets and finally paused and pointed ahead. "We're roughly in the middle of the docks. The ship should pull in soon. It was seen farther up the river a while ago."

Before them was the terminal building and on the opposite side, they could see the lights of the docking space. Tanyith thanked him and launched himself into the air, followed immediately by Fyre. She sighed, not willing to try her indifferent abilities at force flying on such an important occasion, and headed forward to find a good place to climb. When she reached the wall, a knotted rope slithered down the side, and she used it to ascend quickly. Together, they crossed the roof, careful to avoid all the skylights that might betray their presence, and crouched behind the ornamental ridge that ran along the edge facing the river.

They waited and watched for roughly ninety minutes before the large ship eased alongside the dock. Almost instantly, once it was tied into place, openings appeared in four different areas and cargo and people began to appear. It was one of the most impressive things Cali had ever seen, a bizarre combination of overall order and small-scale chaos. Her glasses turned the entire scene to daylight, so it wasn't difficult to locate the Atlanteans when they made their appearance. A group of them came around one corner of the terminal. They separated and half headed directly toward what looked like a crew gangplank on the far side, while the others followed the direction of the main flow of people disembarking roughly amidships. She pointed it out to Tanyith and he replied, "Now look at the other side."

She did and noticed a small group of people loitering at the end of the terminal building, just outside the pools of light that illuminated the rest of the dock. They appeared human and looked intently at the passengers leaving the ship. She nodded. "Okay, I see them. What are they waiting for?"

He sounded focused and angry. "If I read it right—and I'm not sure that I do—there's a contingent that expects to be picked up. Those are the ones coming through the crew area. But there must be some who still need convincing or who are hiding among the passengers because the second group of Atlanteans is headed toward the middle. I think the woman who almost speared you is with them."

"Good. Maybe I can get payback. What's up with the humans? They have to be Zatoras, right?"

"Or members of a lesser gang hired on or maybe others who sell the people they capture. I don't know. But if your point is that they're probably here to kidnap someone, I would say you're right."

They watched the scene play out below. The first group of Atlanteans did indeed escort a line of folks away from the crew gangplank and disappeared around the corner with them. The ones in the middle waited, occasionally talking to people and pointing them over to a waiting area where one of their members stood. They still couldn't act because there was no indication that anything bad was happening. Everyone seemed fine with the situation.

Tanyith's expression seemed to mirror Cali's growing boredom until raised voices emanated from the center of the docks. A group of people coming off the ship walked quickly away from the waiting gang members and toward where the humans were positioned. When the woman in the suit and her cronies followed them, it was clear that a conflict was imminent. She asked, "Now?"

"Now. Let's go clean up the trash." He nodded, satisfaction in his voice.

He and Fyre leapt from the building, and she ran to where they'd arranged the rope for a speedy descent between illuminated areas. *I really need to work on my entrances.*

CHAPTER TWENTY-SEVEN

Tanyith veered toward the Atlanteans, so Cali approached the humans. *Maybe it has something to do with his cover story. Or maybe he simply wants revenge. Either way, I won't argue.* She stayed near the terminal building and tried to get close before they noticed she was there. Ahead and to the right, the four Atlanteans—two women and two children, it appeared from this distance—continued to move in the direction of the darkness at the edge to avoid the entreaties of the Atlantean gang members.

At a loud honking behind her, she twisted her head as a large semi-trailer stopped next to the cargo gangway. There were already pallets on the way to it. She didn't know much about how that kind of thing worked, but she'd thought the existence of the terminal building, with its docks on the opposite side sized properly for the big vehicles to pull up to, meant that the truck shouldn't be there. She shrugged, dismissed it, and focused instead on the four—no, there were six now, with another six about a hundred yards behind but moving in the same direction—humans in front of her.

She waved at Fyre, who dipped a wing to acknowledge the gesture and pointed at the trailing half-dozen. He swooped in that direction, and she put them from her mind, knowing he'd at least delay them and probably take them out of the fight altogether. The rest were on an intercept course and sauntered without apparent intent on a trajectory to meet the Atlantean newcomers outside the lit area of the docks. She charted her own path to intercept them about three-quarters of the way there and stepped into the light. It was almost ten seconds before they saw her and the guns appeared. A trio turned toward her and the rest continued toward their prey.

Oh no, you don't. Shouts rang out from behind, considerable swearing punctuated by the word "Dragon." *Go, Fyre, go.* She summoned her full-body force shield and attacked. The gunfire echoed from the buildings but it was far enough away from the main activities that those engaged in cruise ship procedures probably wouldn't notice, which was good for everyone involved. The bullets met her barrier and ricocheted or fell, depending on the angle at which they'd struck it. When they fired dry, the gang members reloaded and holstered the guns. Two of them drew combat batons and the third two large knives. They spread into a semicircle to await her approach.

She had only seconds before she'd reach them, and she wondered if she should focus on the other group instead. Still, there was time as long as she dealt with these quickly, and she didn't want them at her back. She let the shield fall, drew her sticks, and targeted the one on the left with a ferocious grin on her face.

Tanyith had hoped he could reach the gathered enemies without betraying his presence, but they noticed him almost immediately when he broke into a run. As one, they turned and raced across the gangway into the cargo area of the ship. His speed slowed as his brain tried to process that decision, and he decided it didn't matter. *Cali has a handle on protecting the people who came off the ship, so all I need to do is find these jerks and deal with them.* He increased his speed again and his boots rang as they clanged along the metal slab that connected the vessel to the shore.

He launched himself inside when he reached the end of the plank in case they were lying in wait. His path carried him over a forklift and numerous people who moved things with hand jacks and he landed on a stack of plastic-wrapped boxes on a pallet. The free-standing stacks were only about eight feet high, but there was a huge scaffolding system set up deeper in the ship that would allow for several pallets to be slotted in to fill the full height of the four-story area.

A blast of shadow magic struck the side of his support stack, toppled the boxes beneath him, and flung him back. The slide of containers cushioned his fall but it was still an awkward landing, and he smacked his knee hard on the metal deck. He cursed and forced himself into motion in time to avoid the follow-up attack, a line of force that sliced a nearby box in two. Hastily, he summoned a force shield attached to his left forearm and barreled into the open.

Four enemies were in view, including the woman he'd fought in the Atlantean base. He shifted to the side to put one of her people between them and attacked a third who happened to be closest. The man thrust both hands out and a force ball streaked toward him, but he deflected it with his shield, generated a baseball-sized sphere of magical power in his right hand, and lobbed it at the man's knee. It thumped home and his foe fell howling to the floor, clutching the damaged joint. *One down, too many to go.*

He barely raised the shield in time to deflect the spear thrown by the dark-suited woman. It returned to her as she advanced toward him with all the confidence and inevitability of Arnold Schwarzenegger's Terminator.

Cali had intended to charge past the man and put him between her and his allies, but he stepped away to force her inside. She skittered sideways at a different target—the one with the knives. Her left stick chopped in and he managed to catch it on crossed blades, but the kick that channeled all her momentum into his stomach catapulted him away and out of the fight. His weapons clattered noisily when they fell.

She paid for the attack with a blow in the lower back from the middle man's baton. Fortunately, she'd maintained her forward motion so its impact was blunted, but it was still enough to drag a cry of pain past her gritted teeth. She spun to her right and lashed out blindly with that stick to drive him away. It caught nothing but air as he backpedaled. Her desire to pursue was thwarted by the third man, her original target, who waded in with his own sticks flying.

They traded strikes and blocks, evenly matched enough that neither could get through the other's defenses with a decisive blow. She tried aiming at his fingers, but he was wise to the trick and almost snuck a shot through to her face in return. When she backed away slowly, hoping to draw him forward, he followed and she suppressed a smile and focused on the cadence. At exactly the right moment, she hurled her right stick at the remaining man, who had attempted to sneak in from that side, then slipped ahead and to the left. She caught her foe's wrist as his strike flashed past her and yanked him forward to break his balance, skipped back, and used the joint as a lever. Faced with the choice of a broken wrist or going with the motion, he chose the latter and she flipped him easily. She pistoned a foot into the nerve bundle in the side of his leg, knowing it would numb the limb and keep him out of the fight for a time.

If he's smart, he'll limp the hell away from here. She caught movement in her peripheral vision and whipped her left stick around to redirect the blow that arced down at her head far enough aside to miss her. *Damn. I wish Sensei Ikehara had seen that. It's evidence that I've actually learned something in our training sessions.* She launched a sidekick into the man's exposed ribs and followed it with baton blows to each of his knees when he doubled over. He fell, too, and she raised a hand to summon her thrown weapon. She turned in a circle and noticed an odd reflection in the distance. When she squinted and stared at it for a moment, she realized it was one of the enemies the Draksa had been fighting, frozen in place, and smiled at the prowess of her partner. *Now, where did the rest of those idiots get to?*

Tanyith wanted nothing more than to confront the woman who had almost impaled him twice, but her allies swarmed around and there was no way he could handle them all at once. He blasted one and then another with bursts of force that thrust them back but not out while he raced deeper into the storage area and finally ducked out of the line of sight behind a series of stacked pallets. In the increased darkness, the image in his glasses shifted to provide both the brighter view they'd displayed but also a smear of color that represented body heat.

It was the only thing that saved him from the veiled attacker who crept over the pallet beside him. His illusion was flawless with not even a visual ripple, but he hadn't thought to mask his temperature. As he pounced, Tanyith avoided the tackle by taking a quick step away and blasted an upward kick toward the man's groin. The assailant grunted and crumpled despite the hard plastic his foot had connected with, and while he was down, a follow-up kick drove into his temple.

The noise revealed his position, though—or the man had told them—because suddenly, he was confronted by two of his enemies. He summoned a force shield barely in time to block the shadow and flame that boiled out at him and ran forward to thrust the barrier into them. They fell back, but he screamed when the damned woman's spear cut a line of fire across his calves. If she'd been a little lower, she would have nailed his Achilles and a little higher would have unstrung his knees. He said a prayer of thanks as he launched himself upward on a pillar of force and toward the door to the outside. *I only need a second to take a potion. Then, we'll continue this dance, you wench.*

Cali neared the trio who had focused on the Atlanteans when they were still twenty feet from their target. She risked a blast of force to carry her up and over them and twisted as she landed to create alarm in the newcomers and elicit curses from her enemies. She gestured at the gangsters. "How about you boys turn around and go home? These folks don't seem to want your attention."

They looked at each other, and the center person said, "You should stay with your own gang, witch. Your magic won't help you three on one."

She grinned and thrust her hands out to spear the speaker with twin blasts of force, one aimed at his groin and the other at his solar plexus. They arrived simultaneously and she caught a glimpse of his shocked face for only a second before he careened ten feet away to land in a crumpled heap. She called, "I think you counted wrong." The two in front of her drew pistols, and she leapt back and conjured a wide force shield to cover herself and the foursome behind her. "Get out. I'll take care of these two idiots. Stay out of their firing lanes."

An acknowledgment sounded from behind, and she

surged into an attack. She realized she'd screwed up when one of them shot the ground in front of her and the ricochet bounced up under the imperfectly positioned shield and sliced into her leg. The limb collapsed beneath her and she rolled to the side in pain, barely managing to reposition the shield to catch the rounds that followed. When their guns clicked empty, one raced at her while the other started to reload.

She let the shield fade and dispatched a burst of force at the one with the weapon. It didn't hit him but did explode a light over his head, and the falling glass drove him away. *Great. Good aim, Cali.* She pushed herself to her feet as the other man arrived and threw a punch at her head. A hop to the side with her weight on her good leg took her out of range, and he lashed out with a kick that knocked it out from under her. She fell again, and he stood over her with a mocking expression as he raised a foot to stamp on her face.

Fyre appeared to be angry because instead of freezing the man, he flew directly into him, dug his claws into the enemy's shoulders, and lifted him. His roar overpowered the man's scream of agony, and his strong wings flapped once, twice, then again as he rocketed toward the side of a building. The Draksa released the man and pulled up into a loop. His victim barely managed to curl to protect his head before he pounded into the structure and fell the dozen feet to the ground. He didn't move at all.

Cali realized she'd watched instead of acting when she heard the click of a pistol being primed to shoot. She pushed the idea of protection to the front of her mind and whispered, "*Aspida,*" and a barrier sprung to life around her. She curled inside it to wait out the attack, felt the warmth of the blood flowing from her wounded leg into her boot, and hoped he'd fire fast enough that she could swallow a potion before she passed out.

Tanyith made it outside safely and landed on top of the eighteen-wheeler parked at the dock. He turned to face the ship, ready for the woman to make an appearance so he could blast her back into it and eliminate the other Atlanteans. *It's cool. We've got this.* The falsehood of his self-congratulation was revealed when the rear doors of the trailer opened and a flood of Atlanteans in matching hoodies and masks flooded out. His brain refused to accept what his eyes told him, and in the moment when he was distracted, an attack from inside the ship hurled him from his perch.

CHAPTER TWENTY-EIGHT

The thought flitted across Tanyith's mind that he was really tired of being airborne because of others' efforts. In the next moment, he twisted to protect himself from a painful landing on the street with a flexible bubble of force that absorbed the impact. He scrambled to his feet and stared at the people who flowed from the ship in military fatigues, body armor, and rifles. There were dozens more, at least, all looking like they were ready to form a beachhead to invade the city. *What the hell is going on here?*

He ran out of time to worry about the bigger picture when a trio of Atlantean warriors came around one side of the truck and two more around the other. While he fired force blasts as fast as he could, he backpedaled and dodged incoming bursts of shadow and fire. Lightning stabbed in and wreathed him in burning incandescence and his muscles spasmed when the energy surged into them. He screamed in rage and pain and launched himself upward to escape the follow-up assault, aiming for the roof of the terminal building. His trajectory was far from perfect and instead of landing cleanly, he collided with one of the skylights, fell through, and barely maintained the presence of mind to throw another force bubble to cushion his fall. When he landed, he blacked out.

Cali heard a loud noise from the direction of the cruise ship—like a whole group of people had screamed at once—but couldn't focus her attention to find out what was going on. Fyre had disabled the man shooting at her with an ice blast and she'd drunk the healing potion, which had instantly tried to put her to sleep. She guzzled the blue energy liquid and stood unsteadily, trembling as her flesh knitted itself together and happy to discover she could now stand on her formerly wounded leg.

When her vision cleared, she initially thought she was hallucinating. The sheer number of people who streamed out of the ship made no sense, nor did the outfits they wore. She gaped as the men and women—who looked military—confronted the Atlantean gang members, some with the guns they carried, and others with fists and knives. She peered around to ensure no one was near enough to threaten her, then realized she didn't know what to do.

Fyre screeched over her head and flew toward the terminal building, then turned and returned to her and repeated the process. *Damn, we need telepathy. Or radios.* She jogged after him and he seemed content. They'd covered only a few yards when something entirely unexpected happened. A helicopter swooped in and hovered over the docks, its blades barely clearing the high points on the terminal roof. Four figures leapt out clad in identical dark clothing and body armor. One, about half the size of the others, had shockingly purple hair in the spotlight that shone down from the aircraft. That one, together with two more, slid down black lines, while the fourth clearly used magic to slow their descent.

When they landed, the new arrivals immediately engaged the people in the camouflage uniforms. Cali pointed upward to tell Fyre to check the roof, then lost sight of the bigger battle when she crossed into the terminal building. In the center, Tanyith lay on his back with a number of enemies closing in on him. She attacked them from behind, blasted two with bursts of force that knocked them into the others, and raced in to stand beside her ally. "Get up."

He shook his head and said groggily, "I can't."

She risked a look and saw nothing broken on his body. "Yes, you can. Stand your lazy ass up right now, Tanyith."

With a moan, he staggered to his feet and put a hand on her shoulder to steady himself. They were in the middle of an empty space and enemies surrounded them on three sides. As one, they retreated in the only possible direction, moving toward the large scaffolded storage area that ran through the center of the building and would prevent them from reaching the other side. The woman in the suit from the battle at the nightclub appeared behind their other enemies. Again, she was dressed impeccably, this time in a dark navy-blue suit and matching shirt and tie. all one color but attractive nonetheless. Her hair was slightly mussed, and Cali considered mentioning it but the woman spoke first.

"We're here for him, Ms Leblanc. You're free to go."

She shook her head. "I don't know what you are all up to out there with all the chaos and guns and stuff, but there's no way you'll get to him without going through me first."

The other woman frowned. "That's inconvenient but acceptable." A surprisingly gentle burst of force knocked Cali a step to the side and suddenly, she was trapped as four enemies placed walls of magical power around her. She could see them maintain the spells while the woman moved toward her target. The barrier didn't prevent her from seeing or hearing clearly.

He snarled outrage. "What is it with you people?"

She shrugged. "You are a thorn in our side. From what I'm told, you always were."

Tanyith shook his head. "When I was part of the gang, we cared about the Atlantean people."

She gave a dismissive laugh. "You lacked vision and still do. When we're done, the Atlantean people in New Orleans will be much better off."

Cali called out a warning as the gang member behind the woman shifted position, but the leader raised her hand and stopped their motion. She looked over her shoulder and ordered them to back off. They complied and she held a palm out and the magical spear that was the only weapon they'd seen her use appeared in it. She nodded at Tanyith. "I will give you the honor of single combat in recognition of the fact that you were once one of us and, as deluded as you were and are, you still considered the future of our people as your chief concern. Do you accept?"

She wanted to tell him not to do it but there were really no other options. *I'll find a way out of here, and I'll show her exactly how much I respect rules set by a gangster.*

Tanyith drew his right-hand Sai and summoned a shield onto his left forearm. The woman's subordinates pushed pallets aside magically to create a rough circle, similar to those used for ritual combat in both New and old Atlantis. She wove the spear in an eloquent figure of eight in front of her, and he was forced to acknowledge that every movement she made was incredibly graceful. *Damn, maybe Sienna's right and I was in prison for too long.*

He laughed at himself. *Sure, she wants to kill you, but maybe you could do an enemies to lovers thing, right?* He shook his head at his own stupidity and pulled on his game face as he circled with her and pushed his aches and pains to the back of his brain. The spear licked out at his eyes and he leaned back. It stopped short when he positioned the shield in the way. She stepped in and twirled the other end up between his legs, and he caught it in the curved guard of his sai before it struck. He whipped the shield around, hoping she'd push in to try to force past his guard, but she backpedaled and circled again.

Dammit, she's all cold logic and strategy. The look on her face reinforced the conclusion, as she didn't seem particularly excited to fight him or even particularly annoyed. It wasn't a reaction he usually engendered in people, as he tended to be polarizing. It would make forcing her into a mistake exceptionally difficult. *Okay, let's change it up then.* He rushed at her and cursed the pain in his calves that stole some of his speed. With the shield, he hammered the weapon aside when she tried to impale him, then swung the sai in a feint. She opened slightly to block it, and he thrust forward, knees-first. Her eyes widened when he careened into her blocking arm and shoved her back.

She stumbled and went down and he landed on top of her. His initial attack was an elbow blow, but her raised arms blocked it. He pushed up and let his weight fall on her again, but she accepted the impact without reacting. It only became apparent that she'd locked his wrist out when his sai began to move toward his face. He dropped it, and she used the hand that had controlled the limb to punch him in the temple. The blow caused him to shift to one side, and a surge of motion from below threw him off in that direction. He scrambled to his feet in time to evade the point of the spear as it sought his heart.

Blood trickled down his cheek and his head was ringing. For the first time in the fight, he thought it was more likely that he'd lose than that he'd win, and he glanced around reflexively for ways to escape. When his brain began to function again, he remembered Cali was trapped nearby. There was no way he would abandon her. *So, how do I beat this wench?* She attacked and he blocked again, but his arms felt heavy as the pain in his skull increased.

A sudden shout shattered the moment and the enemies who had maintained the barrier around his partner scattered when Fyre bulldozed through their ranks. He froze one who had moved too slowly to evade his attack and grasped another in his claws. Cali appeared at a run from the side and his opponent dropped and rolled away to avoid the surprise attack. He expected the enemy leader to continue the fight but instead, she snarled and ran. A moment later, two dark-uniformed people he hadn't seen before rushed into the room and engaged the half-dozen enemies who remained. The taller one—a woman with black hair—mixed magical attacks and punches that made loud snaps when they connected. The shorter one was a shockingly unexpected purple-haired troll. Equally surprising was the way he used two combat batons to disable his share of the Atlanteans.

In moments, the area was clear and the duo raced out through the opening that faced the docks. Fyre landed beside Cali with a fluttering of his wings, then folded them back carefully along his body. She reached out a hand and petted him absently.

Tanyith looked at her, and she stared at him. "So...uh, this turned out really different than I thought it would."

She laughed. "Right? I guess we should be used to that by now or something." She twisted her head to look in the direction the strangers had gone. "They came in by heli-copter but I have no idea why. There were a couple more of them, though. That was a troll, right? I've never seen one in person."

He nodded, then realized she wasn't looking at him and replied, "Yeah. Definitely a troll."

"I thought they were small. Or really big."

"They can be many different sizes, according to what I've heard. But my knowledge is minimal."

Cali shrugged. "I guess we should see what's going on outside. I kind of don't want to, though."

He laughed. "I know how you feel. But we need to make sure that no one who wasn't here to fight was hurt. Do you still have a healing potion left?"

"Nope. I used it."

Tanyith grimaced. "Okay, I'll hold on to mine, then, in case we find wounded. But if I collapse, you'll have to carry me."

"I've more or less carried you the whole time I've known you. Why should today be different?" She strode toward the door with the Draksa at her side, and he was fairly sure she walked faster than usual, doubtless only to tweak him. He sighed, shook his head, and followed.

CHAPTER TWENTY-NINE

C ali stared in surprise when she exited the terminal building onto the docks. What had seemed like a chaotic battlefield when she went inside had transformed into a space of extreme order. Police cars flashed red and blue at each end of the lit-up area near the cruise ship, and a line of men and women bound with zip ties sat in the middle of the wide zone.

Weapons had been piled on the far side, presumably taken from the military-looking people. *How long was I trapped for? Sheesh.* Her review of the situation was interrupted by the appearance of a familiar face. Detective Barton grinned at her. "Well, look at that. Massive fighting involving gang members and who do I see but the perennially uninvolved Caliste Leblanc."

She snorted at her. "Right. So surprising that I'm exactly where you told me to be. What a shocker."

The other woman laughed. "I'm only messing with you. I'm glad to see you're safe." She looked past her with a smile. "That goes for you, too, but less, Shale."

Tanyith sounded tired. "That is not my name anymore."

"Are you both okay?"

Cali nodded. "Never better. What went on here?"

Barton shrugged. "I'm still trying to find out. What we know for sure is that the night started exactly like we all thought it would. The Atlantean gang came to meet some people who were clearly expecting to see them. My officers watched them all leave fairly quickly after the ship docked and followed."

"Yeah, we were watching them too. But what's with the rest?"

"It looks as if the human gang tried to intercept some of them—maybe to replace the ones who miraculously escaped." She stared into Cali's eyes and shrugged at the lack of confirmation. "Clearly, there were some small-scale skirmishes. Anyway, things went to hell when the mercenaries attacked the Atlantean gang, who had apparently brought more people than expected. I truly know zero about that, but my superiors will work hard to find answers."

She grinned. "So you'll tell us what you learn?"

The detective shook her head. "Not likely, unless you have something to trade for it." She waved and walked off to intercept an officer who jogged across the space.

Tanyith quipped, "Why can't you two get along?"

Cali shrugged. "Mainly because she's so distracted by you that she's not logical. Seriously, you two should simply date and be done with it." Her heart wasn't in the teasing, though, because she continued to scan the area. It wasn't clear what she was looking for, but when she saw the troll and the woman who had been with him, she decided they were it. "Come on, you two."

As they approached, it became clear that the two were talking to another person and the third member of the trio turned out to be Nylotte. Cali nudged Tanyith, and he glanced up and said, "Well, she did say she'd be nearby. Maybe she knows what the hell went on."

When they arrived, the Drow stared at them and snapped at her partner, "Are you simply going to limp around all night or will you take your potion?" He looked like he wanted to reply but clearly thought better of it and sipped from the red cylinder.

The athletic-looking brunette laughed and extended her hand to Cali. "I saw your attack when the box fell. Nice job. I'm Diana Sheen. The half-pint next to me is Rath."

The troll grinned at her and said, "We are the law." His companion rolled her eyes.

"Cali Leblanc. The guy with me is Tanyith. The short one is Fyre." Handshakes were exchanged, and Rath offered them fist-bumps in turn. "I guess you know Nylotte?"

Diana laughed. "Oh, you could say that. She's a friend but more importantly, she's my teacher in all things magic."

Tanyith grinned. "So, are you being punished for something? What did you do wrong?"

The Drow rolled her eyes as Diana joined the laughter. "She's much worse when you get to know her. She's probably been on her best behavior with you. I take it you're the one she rescued from Trevilsom?"

He nodded. "And I'll owe her forever."

The Drow waved it away. "That particular account is closed. And actually, Diana here owes both of you, now."

Cali tilted her head. "Why?"

The woman twisted to face her, and Cali noticed that a hilt protruded over her shoulder. *Okay, guns and a sword. That's weird.* "It would be a really long and ridiculously involved story, so I'll summarize it. Basically, we had word that there was a human criminal organization that was looking to exterminate a group of magicals in New Orleans. When Nylotte mentioned that you were investigating a cruise ship that was of interest to a magical group in the city, it struck my team that maybe the things were related."

She nodded. "That makes sense."

Diana continued, "So, my techs did a little hacking and we discovered both a money trail leading back to the Zatora crime syndicate here and an unscheduled stop on the ship's itinerary. We put two and two together and sent drones in to take a look. The idiots tied up over there are cheap mercenaries who were hired to wipe out the Atlanteans here. But it turns out there was an extra bonus. The additional gang members were here to offload a shipment of explosives from the ship."

Tanyith whistled. "That's a lucky find. Why didn't they bring them in by portal?"

She shrugged. "Honestly? I have no idea. Maybe they didn't come from New Atlantis but somewhere else along the way where they don't have anything set up. It's not how I would have done it but sometimes, even the smartest people make mistakes."

Nylotte nodded. "Sometime, when you have a week or two, I can tell you about all the screwups Diana has managed since we met. It's quite an exhaustive list."

Again, Diana rolled her eyes, but the smile on her lips clearly revealed her affection for the Drow. "So I guess she's right. We wouldn't have been in the right place at the right time without your help. It's my expectation that this will turn out to be a piece of something bigger, which means my team has a leg up on something we'd probably wind up dealing with anyway."

"Your team?" Cali asked. "Who the heck are you people?"

The woman laughed. "That's a little uncertain at the moment. We used to be a federal agency tasked with the protection of a given territory from magical criminals. That went a little sideways and now, we're more of a self-determined organization but still focused on things magical and answerable to the United States government."

"Do you have investigators on your team?"

"Yep. We didn't bring our primary one with us on this adventure, but he was a detective for many years before he joined us. Plus, everyone has some basic skills in our previous careers."

Tanyith laughed. "Are you thinking of joining up, Cali?"

"If it'll get me away from you, show me where to sign," she quipped,

There was a laugh from behind as another woman in dark body armor pushed through. She had long black hair, dark eye makeup, and perfect lips. Where the other woman looked like someone you'd see in real life, this one could have been a model. *Or a recruiting poster.* "Okay, boss, it looks like we have this place locked down. They'll quarantine the ship until Glam and her bots can give it a proper search."

Diana nodded. "Cali, Tanyith, and Fyre, this is Cara, my second in command."

Cali laughed. "Wait, you have a team with two women in charge? Seriously now, where do I sign up?"

Cara smiled and replied, "Skill is the only thing that matters to us. If you have the credentials, we could certainly talk about it sometime."

Her boss shook her head. "But now is not that time. We need to get a move on." She turned to Nylotte. "Do you have a suggestion for where we can portal to in the city? It'd be more convenient than using the jet or helicopters if we have to pursue investigations here."

"I can help with that," Cali interrupted. "I mean, I could help with the investigation, but that's not what I was referring to. My boss, Zeb, could probably be convinced to let you use the basement of his business as a landing location."

Diana looked at the Drow, who gave her a nod. "That sounds good. How about we go and meet him?" She turned to Cara. "You and Hercules wrap things up here and head back. Rath and I will go check Cali's place." The other woman nodded and headed off, and the team leader asked her teacher, "Are you coming along?"

She sighed. "Given your lack of ability with people, I probably should." Diana laughed, as she had at all the Drow's sharp-tongued comments. Rath and Fyre stood from where they'd played some kind of game involving batting an object that looked very much like a grenade between them.

Cali summoned a portal. She couldn't hold back a laugh when the troll did a series of flips and launched himself into it, and she followed them through with a wide grin. *This is absolutely the weirdest night ever.*

CHAPTER THIRTY

It had taken Usha an hour to calm Danna's anger over the events at the docks before she sent the woman to seek information on the results of the evening's activities. Her subordinate was most upset over her own inability to eliminate the thorn that irritated them all but was also irate over the unexpected attack by the mercenaries the Zatoras had hired.

Danna had texted shortly after her departure with confirmation that it had been the syndicate. They had picked up one of their middle-level people off the streets and tortured him until he confessed. The enforcer, who still lived, had apparently proven quite adept at breaking bones in what appeared to have been the most agonizing way possible. While she was aware that information gleaned in that fashion was often unreliable, she had confidence in what she'd heard.

Given the successes they'd had, it made sense that the human gang would have to act and do so decisively. How they knew about the ship—and most concerning, about that particular shipment of goods from the Empress—she didn't know. Danna had vowed to find the answer for her. As if the thought had summoned her, Usha's second in command entered the office and joined her on the couch. She waited to be addressed before speaking, as always.

"What news?"

She smoothed her tie under her unbuttoned suit jacket. "All but nine have reported in. We are investigating whether those still missing are dead, imprisoned, or captured. The docks are still on lockdown, though, so information is difficult to come by."

Usha nodded. "We need better people in the police department and maybe in the city government. Look into that."

"I will. We secured additional confirmation that the mercenaries were hired by the Zatoras using the tip the captive provided about how they were paid. They went cheap."

She laughed. "That describes our friend Rion Grisham well. He thinks he's a classic gangster when in fact, he's a jumped-up lieutenant at best. He doesn't know that when you attack first, you need to strike hard enough that your opponent can't get up. We'll make sure he learns that lesson well."

Danna smiled. "I look forward to being a part of that."

"You will be. Now, what of the people in the black uniforms?"

She scowled. "I can't find any information about them at all. They're like ghosts. No one has seen them or heard of them. We scoured the Internet and found some stories by searching for a purple-haired troll but even then, they were inconclusive and nothing more than rumors."

The corners of Usha's mouth turned down. "That's not a good sign for our future endeavors. Perhaps we'll be lucky and discover that they're after the Zatoras but somehow, I don't imagine that will be the case. Since they were seen using magic, we must assume they might be interested in us."

"It is always safest to be paranoid."

"Agreed. Finally, then, what of Tanyith and Caliste?"

Danna sighed. "If not for the girl's interference, I would have killed him before the woman and the troll interfered."

Usha patted her subordinate's leg. "Let it go. There will be another chance. What do you suggest we do about them going forward?"

She shrugged. "The girl was promised a week of preparation time. There are still several days left of that. In the meantime, we should scour the city, try to find out where their base is aside from the tavern and the dojo, and make sure we get and keep eyes on them. It might be best to synchronize the next attacks so they can't warn one another."

"What pairing do you suggest?"

"It seems unlikely that we can separate the woman and her dog. So that will need to be the pair on her side."

Usha raised an eyebrow. "Clearly, it is not a dog."

Danna nodded. "Yeah. I know. But we're still not sure exactly what it is. Magical, almost certainly, since the girl can't be powerful enough yet to maintain that veil while doing other things. The creature must be doing it for her.

Plus, it keeps changing color." She laughed softly. "It really is a shame we can't get her on our side."

"Maybe once Tanyith is dealt with and if she survives the next round, we can try to recruit her."

"Voluntarily?"

The leader shrugged. "Or involuntarily. Perhaps her karate teacher or the tavern owner would be enough to convince her. Or one of the people she plays with in Jackson Square."

Danna sighed. "I really don't think it will work, but I agree that it has to be tried. The last issues are with the drug distribution. We have the one for the humans ready."

"Excellent. Let's start right on the border with the Zatoras, everywhere our territories connect. If we can drum up a demand from their side of the lines, it should weaken them and strengthen us. Even better, we might find someone who's on the inside, which will make everything easier."

Her second recognized her words for the dismissal they were and departed without responding. Usha drummed her fingers on the back of the couch and wondered what else they could do to convince Leblanc to join them. If she did survive the coming attack, it would speak volumes about her abilities and to add the girl to her team would be an unprecedented coup. Surely, the Empress would reward her magnificently if she could only pull it off. It might even be enough to get her a seat on her council of advisors.

She fell asleep with that image in her mind and dreamed of ways to turn Caliste to the cause of her people.

CHAPTER THIRTY-ONE

After the adventures of the previous evening, Cali slept until it was time to leave for work at the Drunken Dragons. She wandered around more or less in a daze and told Zeb the whole story when she had moments to spare. He'd heard part of it the night before when he'd agreed to let Sheen and her team use the basement as a portal location and provided the magical extras that would let them pass through the wards built into the place. She'd explained to Diana that she should be honored since most didn't have that privilege.

Toward the end of the evening, Tanyith showed up for a quick drink. He was dressed for his date with Sienna and looked charmingly nervous about the whole thing. She decided not to tease him but only wished him good fortune and went about her business. Once he departed, she took a seat across the bar from Zeb. "Do you think the date will go well for him?"

Her boss shrugged. "There's no way to tell. People change, and the time in prison no doubt turned him into a very different person. It might be a better fit or might be worse. It's good that he hasn't shied away from finding the answer, though."

She nodded. "On another topic, did you discuss last night's events with any of your friends?"

"Yeah, a couple. They were as surprised as we all were. There was no hint that the Zatoras might try something that audacious." He shook his head. "Life's never dull in the Big Easy, right?"

Cali laughed. "That's certainly one way to put it." She scowled as someone called her name and yelled, "In a minute." She grinned at Zeb. "I love messing with them. But hey, if you could ask around to see who knows about weird languages and symbols, that would be awesome."

He shook his head and sighed. "You need to go to the library. I'll let Scoppic know you'll stop by on Sunday afternoon."

She began to protest but his raised eyebrow stopped her. *Fine. I have a ton of questions begging for answers, so I might as well dig into them. It's probably a safe place to avoid the gang's next attack, too.* "Okay. Magical library. Sunday. Got it." She turned and muttered, "Emalia's right, there are no damn shortcuts to be had in this life." Another voice called her name and she yelled, exasperated, "Shut it! I'm on my way!"

He had expected that she might cancel, but his date agreed to return to town for the occasion. Tanyith escorted Sienna into a booth on the far right of the Stallion Bar. It had seemed appropriate for them to have their night out here, the place indirectly responsible for the opportunity. She slid in first and he moved to the other side. They ordered drinks—both chose Manhattans—and he asked her to select all their food exactly like it used to be.

She perused the menu with a smile and selected an oyster appetizer—half-raw for her, half-barbecued for him —and a chicken entrée and a pasta dish for them to share. They talked about history until the meals arrived and the conversation turned serious. He explained how sorry he was about her house, and she told him it didn't matter, that insurance would cover it, and besides, she needed to redecorate anyway. She told it well, but he knew it was a lie.

The night of the attack had been a turning point, even though neither of them had necessarily realized it at the time. While Sienna was willing to be with someone who wasn't entirely legal, she had no desire to be a part of that world directly, and the violence and mental baggage of the event at her house had obviously affected her deeply. He saw it in her struggle to stay relaxed, in the way she held her drink, and in the slight downturn at the corners of her mouth.

He made his best effort to keep the conversation light and pleasant. When dessert arrived, he focused on watching her eat and on giving himself good memories to add to the mental scrapbook with all the other ones they'd shared. He touched her hand. "This was lovely, but it's not there for you, I think. Am I right?"

She nodded. "You are. I thought maybe I could find it, but there's too much history. Too much stuff." He knew she was referring both to the distant past and more recent events.

"Well then. Friends it is."

With a smile, he raised his glass in a toast and she clinked it. "Friends. Always."

He'd expected that he would feel sad, but it was okay. There was some regret but nothing critical. *Maybe it wasn't right for me either. Besides, who has time for a relationship, anyway?* He grinned at her. "So. Let's talk strategy for tracking down the idiot who disappeared on you."

The challenges continue! Join Cali, Fyre and her magical band of outcasts as they continue facing the challenges that come their way in Bewitched Alley Blues.

If you enjoyed this book, you may also enjoy the first series from T.R. Cameron, also set in the Oriceran Universe. The Federal Agents of Magic series begins with Magic Ops and it's available now at Amazon and through Kindle Unlimited.

FBI Agent Diana Sheen is an agent with a secret...

...She carries a badge and a troll, along with a little magic.

But her Most Wanted List is going to take a little extra effort.

She'll have to embrace her powers and up her game to take down new threats,

Not to mention deal with the troll that's adopted her.

All signs point to a serious threat lurking just beyond sight, pulling the strings to put the forces of good in harm's way.

Magic or mundane, you break the law, and Diana's gonna find you, tag you and bring you in. Watch out magical baddies, this agent can level the playing field.

It's all in a day's work for the newest Federal Agent of Magic.

Available now at Amazon and through Kindle Unlimited

AUTHOR NOTES - TR CAMERON

NOVEMBER 10, 2019

Thank you for reading the second book in the *Scions of Magic* series! I hope you loved it as much as I loved writing it – and I really dug the events in this book! I am grateful every day for the chance to share stories with others who love them as much as I do.

Martha's suggestion that I include some of the characters from my other Oriceran series (Diana, Cara, and Rath) was so much fun! I enjoyed kind of seeing them from the outside, through Cali's eyes. Hopefully you enjoyed them, too. Maybe Cali should become an agent? Guess we'll see where things go!

Quick shout out to the beta readers who made the first book so much better. They really came through with a bunch of stuff that I was just too close to the story to see, and in doing so made it so much better.

When I started the series, I didn't have the character of the Empress among my initial ideas. She's really become interesting, to me and hopefully to you, and will probably feature heavily in the second arc (books 5-8). It seems like she's got a lot of potential depth, plus a reason to wind up on the wrong side of the heroes!

I'm gearing up for the 20booksto50k conference in Vegas. It's the premiere indie author event, and I've been attending since the first one in 2017. This one will have TRIPLE the amount of people as that initial gathering, I believe, which is really saying something!

I'm an avid gamer in my occasional spare time, and I've been spending time that I should probably be spending on work playing *Outer Worlds*. So far, it's big fuTn. Still counting the days to season four of the *Expanse*. And I just introduced my daughter to the Matrix, which is something I've been wanting to do since she was born. Very positive response, making me very happy!

My life is uncommonly busy at the moment, with strange and unexpected tasks appearing as if from nowhere. I'm looking deeply forward to the chance to surround myself with other authors and get my brain on straight again. And then it's on to the craziness and fun of the holidays!

My grandmother died recently, with fairly little drama, at 95 years old. I can't even imagine the changes she saw in her life, from beginnings as one of seven children whose father went out for coffee one day and never came back. She worked at a University for a lot of years, running a dining hall and making generations of students happy. Some of my fondest memories are spending summers there with her. Near the end her brain was losing its fight with Alzheimer's, but she still managed to be cheerful and caring most of the time. I'm sad she's gone, but glad that the pain and confusion won't afflict her anymore. And it reminds me to grab onto each moment with my family and wring every last drop of love out of it. Definitely something I'm going to do this celebration season!

My next read is going to be Michael Anderle's *Obsidian Detective.* I loved *Blade Runner*, and the book's ambiance hearkens back to that. November 2019 is also the month the film was set in, so it's doubly appropriate!

Until next time, Joys upon joys to you and yours – so may it be.

Oh, and if you enjoyed this book, please consider leaving a review. Thanks!

PS: If you'd like to chat with me, here's the place. I check in daily or more: .

For more info on my books, and to join my reader's group, please visit www.trcameron.com.

Stay up to date on new releases and fan pricing by signing up for my newsletter. CLICK HERE TO JOIN.

Or visit: www.trcameron.com/Oriceran to sign up.

So, we're cruising toward the end of the year – and the start of a new decade. Both for me and for the planet. I turned 60 this year and we're all heading into 2020. My rallying cry for the next year is to do less and create more. I'll explain...

At the start of this year, my goal was to see if I could expand. Maybe create a universe on my own and call it what I wanted (Peabrain... and side note... mixed reception on the name – big love for the books – and let's test if Michael Anderle is reading these notes – he was right...), go to more conferences, create more opportunities. I guess the watchword was... MORE!

And I got more. More staff, more responsibility, more deadlines, more things to do, more travel, more shaking hands, more meetings, more phone calls. Till one day I noticed I was creating less, doing more and not as happy. It's always a good idea to pay attention to who you're dying to emulate. Mine were all authors who seemed to have more time to contemplate what they wanted to put on a page. You know... write.

I think the best moment was when I was doing daily Facebook Live readings of books that were coming out that week with a throwback oldie on Fridays and I was doing timed sprints with another author, Charley Case who's in the new universe, Terranavis (more on that in a second), and answering a few emails so I wouldn't forget or nothing slipped through the cracks. Sprints, by the way, are when you go for 30 or 40 minutes writing as fast as you can, take a break for 10 minutes and then do it again. No social media, no phone calls, no nothing during that sprint. I did the best I could under the circumstances. And Charley and I took turns keeping time.

But for some reason on this particular day, I was the timer and I remembered to set the timer on my phone – good first step. Somewhere in there I noticed the time and realized I needed to get on Facebook Live and start reading. Totally forgot about Charley...

Even better, during the live reading the timer went off on my phone and I looked over, turned it off and thought, *What was that about?*

Even better than that, after a while, Charley wondered if I had forgotten about the timer and he took his own break, wandering over to Facebook to take a look around and who should he see LIVE! He even said hello and listened for a few minutes.

We had a good laugh about it after the reading was over.

It was time to simplify and get back to what I love. So, all the series in the new universe I was doing have been merged with LMBPN and have a new name, Terranavis. They even have a Facebook page - https://www.facebook.com/terranavisuniverse/ and a Facebook Group will be coming tomorrow. I shut down a lot of the other things and felt a weight lift off me, and I planned out a sane number of books to write for next year (sane for me, okay, I get it – work in progress).

There's some really good stuff coming out – to start with all those Terranavis books at the end of December, plus some great expansion of Oriceran and a familiar detective and her troll will make a return. Maybe even another new collaborator.

Plus, I'm still sprinting with Charley, but he's agreed to be the permanent timer. I'm timer emeritus. I even got a cool new chair that Charley raved about almost every day for months. It comes Monday. Gotta go. It's been a long day of words and dinner needs to be fixed, before it all starts over tomorrow. Simpler plan though, which will also leave me with more time to chat with all of you. More adventures to follow.

OTHER SERIES IN THE ORICERAN
UNIVERSE:

THE DANIEL CODEX SERIES
I FEAR NO EVIL
THE UNBELIEVABLE MR. BROWNSTONE
ALISON BROWNSTONE
SCHOOL OF NECESSARY MAGIC
SCHOOL OF NECESSARY MAGIC: RAINE CAMPBELL
FEDERAL AGENTS OF MAGIC
SCIONS OF MAGIC
THE LEIRA CHRONICLES
REWRITING JUSTICE
THE KACY CHRONICLES
MIDWEST MAGIC CHRONICLES
SOUL STONE MAGE
THE FAIRHAVEN CHRONICLES

OTHER BOOKS BY JUDITH BERENS

CONNECT WITH THE AUTHORS

TR Cameron Social

Website: www.trcameron.com

Facebook: https://www.facebook.com/AuthorTRCameron

Martha Carr Social

Website: http://www.marthacarr.com

Facebook: https://www.facebook.com/groups/MarthaCarrFans/

Michael Anderle Social

Michael Anderle Social
Website:
http://www.lmbpn.com

Email List:
http://lmbpn.com/email/

Facebook Here: https://www.
facebook.com/TheKurtherianGambitBooks/